---- ★ ----

TAKE ONE

"Sound effects!" she said to herself. Glancing over the row of boxes, she said, "Wood. Metal. Gravel. Sand. For making different kinds of footsteps." She looked at the door. "And a sound effects door, with different kinds of locks and openers to sound like different kinds of doors. Isn't that clever!"

She smiled to herself as she reached over the row of boxes to the door and turned the knob on the dead bolt. The door flew open in her face and she screamed when the man rolled out. He fell and his head cracked Pat's right shoulder and knocked her backwards. He thudded to the floor at her feet. His face crunched in the sand box.

---- ★ ----

Murder Takes Two

BERNIE LEE

W🌐RLDWIDE®

TORONTO • NEW YORK • LONDON
AMSTERDAM • PARIS • SYDNEY • HAMBURG
STOCKHOLM • ATHENS • TOKYO • MILAN
MADRID • WARSAW • BUDAPEST • AUCKLAND

For Helen

MURDER TAKES TWO

A Worldwide Mystery/September 1993

First published by Donald I. Fine, Inc.

ISBN 0-373-26127-6

Printed in U.S.A.

ACKNOWLEDGMENTS

My thanks to Russ Gorsline, Rex Recording; to Richard Paynter, DeLane-Lea Studio; and to Ray Elmes of New Scotland Yard.

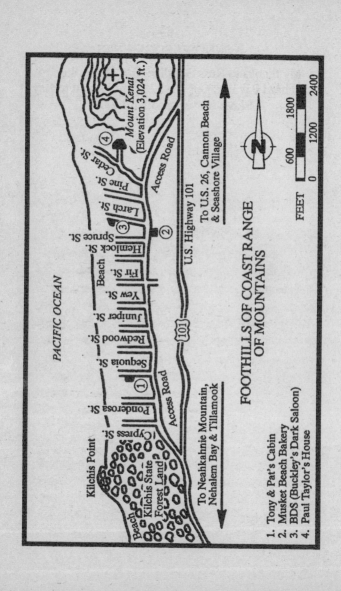

PACIFIC OCEAN

Mount Kenai
(Elevation 3,024 ft.)

Kilchis Point

Beach

Kilchis State
Forest Land

Cypress St.

Ponderosa St.

Sequoia St.

Redwood St.

Juniper St.

Yew St.

Fir St.

Beach

Hemlock St.

Spruce St.

Larch St.

Pine St.

Cedar St.

Access Road

Access Road

U.S. Highway 101

101

To U.S. 26, Cannon Beach
& Seashore Village

To Neahkahnie Mountain,
Nehalem Bay & Tillamook

N

FEET

0   600   1200   1800   2400

FOOTHILLS OF COAST RANGE
OF MOUNTAINS

1. Tony & Pat's Cabin
2. Musket Beach Bakery
3. BDS (Buckley's Dark Saloon)
4. Paul Taylor's House

ONE

Monday Evening, September 6—
London

SHE HAD A strange feeling. It was the first time Pat
had been inside a recording studio. Inside the studio itself. She'd sat in the lobbies of a few studios,
waiting for Tony. And a couple of times after he'd
finished a recording session she'd gone into a control room and he'd introduced her to engineers and
musicians and actors and announcers. But in all the
years she and Tony Pratt had been married, this
was the first time she'd stepped inside where she
could actually *feel* the eerie quiet of a recording
studio. And a *London* recording studio, at that.

The English engineer that Tony was working with
had told Pat about some of the famous actors
who'd been in this studio. She got a kick out of
hearing Eric Richards talk about the radio dramas, plays and sound tracks he'd recorded with
several world-renowned actors. And their famous
names sounded perfectly at home in Eric's broad
British accent. Olivier. Richardson. Guinness.
Burton. The Redgraves, father and daughters. Fa-

mous singers, too. And commercials. He'd mentioned several, familiar to him but unknown to Pat and probably to most of the U.S.

"These days, though, we use this studio primarily for recording music and narration," Eric had told Pat. Then he'd grinned. "But lots and lots of dramas have been performed in here. Spooks and ghosts and bodies galore."

Pat walked slowly across the dark studio in front of the control room. She passed through the wide rectangle of light that beamed down from the control room's wide, double-paned window onto the waxed vinyl floor and bounced up to make a faint yellow-reflection on the ceiling. In a corner beyond the window she saw several microphone stands crowded together like a copse of tiny trees. Their stainless steel trunks reflected the light in tall, thin slivers.

Other than that, the studio was dark. Looking down the long, wide room was like looking into a cave. Except, at the other end, forty or fifty feet away, a circle of light showed through a small round window in the top half of a heavy, air-lock door leading to the front lobby.

Pat turned back toward the light switches on the wall beside the door where she'd come in, at the other end of the control room window. Walking at the edge of the glow spilling out of the control room, she glanced in. Eric stood with his back to the window watching two tape reels revolving slowly on one of the big machines. But where was Tony? He and Pat had come in together, he'd introduced her to Eric, and Eric had showed her into the studio. But where was Tony now? She shrugged. The john, probably.

Eric was listening to music tracks for the television commercials that Tony had written and, from what Tony had said in the past, she knew that the volume inside the soundproof booth was loud enough to wrinkle paint. Out here in the studio, though, the only sound she heard was the sound of her loafers' leather heels on the vinyl floor.

An oddly hollow noise it was, too, alive but at the same time dead. It was almost eerie, the way the sound of her footsteps died against the acoustic tiles lining the tall walls and high ceiling of the soundproof room. There, and gone. A quick death of sound into silence.

Pat smiled, listening to her steps. There and gone, there and—

Suddenly her face froze and she caught her breath. Across the dark studio she heard other footsteps, quiet and quick, almost tiptoe. A chill shivered up her spine.

She stopped. The other footsteps continued. She stared, wide-eyed, and whispered into the dark. "Hello? Who's there?" The quick steps hurried on.

Pat swiveled her head and glared into the control booth. Still no Tony. Just Eric. She spun around again as another sound came out of the shadows.

From far away at the front of the studio she heard a whoosh. The air-lock door at that end moved. A sudden slash of light flashed in. The door opened just a little more. A short, hunched shadow squeezed through, blocked the light for a split second, then was gone as the door sighed shut again.

Pat stood in the dark silence as if petrified. She shivered again and shook her head. "Don't be silly," she muttered to herself. "It's probably just somebody who works here." But she ran to the light switches by the rear studio door. She flipped one, then another and two rows of ceiling lights blinked on and she sagged against the door frame, blowing out a long breath. "There. That's better."

When the lights came on they must have had some effect in the control booth because Eric turned his head and looked over his shoulder toward the studio. He squinted through the glass till he saw Pat, smiled and waved, then turned back to his tapes.

Pat waved back, smiling a fake smile, knowing that he couldn't hear. "*Now* you look around," she grunted. She pushed herself away from the doorway and walked down to the other end of the studio.

At the air-lock door she stood on tiptoe trying to see through the round window. Nothing. She leaned against the metal handle and pushed the heavy door back till it held itself open. She stepped across a short companionway to another heavy door. This one opened into the lobby, and this one, too, she pushed back till it stayed open. She walked through, looked around, saw and heard nothing and nobody.

She continued across the narrow lobby, past the entrance to a corridor of offices, past a small reception desk, to the building's front door. Through the glass she saw early evening light and heard traffic on the busy street.

Pat grabbed the handle and tugged. Locked. A deadbolt. "Huh," she grunted again. "Odd. Either somebody was in and went out and locked it with a key, or somebody is still in." She took a deep breath. "Ohboy." Then she turned and hurried back into the studio, letting the heavy doors swing shut behind her.

As the second door thunked into place, Pat stopped and looked down the length of the studio.

The left side was a long blank wall, bare except for the clusters of electrical outlets near the floor every few feet and, in the far left corner, the grove of microphone stands.

Pat let her gaze continue around from that corner and into the wide, bright window of the control room at the far end of the studio. Eric seemed to be rewinding his tape. Where's Tony, she mumbled at his back. Where have you put my husband?

To the right of the booth was the narrow strip of wall with the light switches, then the door into the corridor, then the corner where that end of the room met the right wall. About ten feet from that corner, toward Pat, a small studio had been built inside the big one. This isolation booth, as Eric had called it, was about eight feet by twelve—about the size of one of the small bedrooms at home.

Tucked into the angle made by the side of the isolation booth and the main wall, and out of sight of the control room, stood a large wood frame. The frame was mounted on casters so that it could be rolled from place to place. Bolted to the frame was a door, an ordinary house door. But running up the edge of the door, one on top of the other, six different kinds of doorknobs and handles had been screwed on. And on the door jamb hung ten different kinds of locks and bolts, from a modern Yale lock to an old-fashioned skeleton-key lock to a sliding bolt to a metal hasp with a wood peg.

A couple of feet in front of the door, six wood boxes were set into the floor, their tops level with it. They were about two feet square. The first square was filled with sand. The next with gravel. The next had a square of slate inset. The next, a square of heavy-looking metal. The next had flooring tile and the last had wood parquet.

Walking slowly toward the corner and the door standing there, Pat looked down at the boxes. In the square containing sand, the surface was scuffed up. A thin layer of sand had spilled out and as Pat passed it her shoes grated on the sandy floor. She heard the sound and stopped. She twisted the sole of her right shoe in the sand and smiled at the sound.

"Sound effects!" she said to herself. Glancing over the row of boxes, she said, "Wood. Metal. Gravel. Sand. For making different kinds of footsteps." She looked at the door. "And a sound effects door, with different kinds of locks and openers to sound like different kinds of doors. Isn't that clever!"

She smiled to herself as she reached over the row of boxes to the door and turned the knob on the deadbolt. The door flew open in her face and she screamed when the man rolled out. He fell and his head cracked Pat's right shoulder and knocked her backwards. He thudded to the floor at her feet. His face crunched in the sand box.

Pat caught her breath and then screamed again. "Tony!" She twisted her head toward the control room and realized that it was still only Eric and that he couldn't hear a thing through the glass. She ran to the window, pounding it with her fists till the vibration or the motion or something caught his attention. Eric turned and jumped when he saw her terrified face.

He ran out of the control room and into the studio. She grabbed his hand and pulled him to the sound effects corner and pointed. Eric looked down at the body, looked at Pat, looked down again and said, "How the hell did *he* get in here?"

At that moment the front air-lock door of the studio opened and Tony walked in.

TWO

The Friday Before the Monday

THE TELEPHONE RANG in the cabin near Musket Beach, Oregon. Tony Pratt, with a mug of hot chocolate in each hand, walked past the phone and through the open front door to the deck. Behind him, his wife Pat stopped at the little table just inside the doorway and picked up the phone. She heard a man's voice talking to someone at the other end. "Hello!" she said.

The man broke off his conversation and said, "Well, I've saved your ass again."

"One moment, please." Pat held the phone out for Tony.

He nodded, traded her a mug of chocolate for the phone, and stepped back inside the cabin. Holding the phone to his ear, all he heard was a crackling sound. "Abe Arthur," he said. "No contest. I'd know that laugh anywhere."

"Your wife is a very sharp lady."

"I know. Where are you?"

"The office, where else?"

"You called from San Francisco to talk about my wife?"

"No."

"You want to hear about the kids, too?"

"No."

"Well, Jenny's a junior at the U. of O. and Dan's at Oregon State, a sopho—"

"I thought you'd stop being such a smartass when you got out of the agency racket. I called to tell you that the video for your TV spots has been dubbed—"

"Good."

"—and that Bonham has copies. I personally put the reel in his briefcase—"

"Good."

"—so now you can catch your flight to London without worrying."

"Good. And thank you."

"Just trying to save you a few more gray hairs. You writers always worry."

"You art directors are always diplomatic."

"It comes from dealing with account executives like Bonham."

Tony paused. "How's Gary getting along? Any better?"

"Not that I can see." Abe Arthur's tone stayed wry and dry. "Still on some kind of downer. Right now, in fact, he's in his office with the door closed.

Again. His secretary says he just sits there and stares out the window."

"Strange."

"Yup."

"I thought this trip to England might snap him out of it, whatever it is."

"Nope."

"Wonder what's bothering him."

"Nobody knows. But there you go all worried again. He'll get over it."

"Maybe. Maybe I can get him to talk about it while we're in London."

"He'll be all right. Relax and enjoy the trip. Pat going with you?"

"Wouldn't go without her."

"Good. She deserves *something* for all the years she's been stuck with you."

"You're a wonderful person, Abe."

Arthur's laugh cackled again and he said, "I know."

"Thanks for calling about the tape."

"Don't mention it. Call me when you get back. Let me know how it goes."

"Will do."

As TONY AND ABE talked, Gary Bonham stared out over San Francisco through the window of his corner office. But he didn't see the city. He listened.

For the tenth time he replayed a tape he'd made thirty minutes earlier, the tape of his client's telephone call from Chicago.

Secretly—only his secretary knew about the small tape recorder in the bottom-left drawer of his desk—Bonham had begun taping all client calls a year earlier, after a near-fatal misunderstanding about a million-dollar television contract.

This latest call, on the surface, was just a normal conversation with Chet Norris of Thomas Baking Company, the largest account in Bonham's agency. Norris was confirming plans to meet on Sunday in London, where recording sessions were scheduled for Monday. But beneath Norris's forced and heavy ribaldry, Bonham heard the threat. Again.

"It's true," Norris had said, "my promotion to Marketing Director brings me a bigger paycheck, but it also increases my expenses." Norris inserted a confidential little chuckle. "I'll have to move into a better apartment, drive a better car, drink a better grade of booze, buy a better class of hookers. You know how that goes. So I'll have to continue to 'augment' my income. You know how that goes, too."

"I think I understand," Bonham's voice answered quietly.

"In fact, I'll have to 'augment' my 'augmentation,' if you follow me."

Meaning you get a bigger kickback, Bonham thought. Aloud he said, "That might be hard to do."

Norris's voice dropped into its deep, confidential tone. "You'll find a way. You always do. Incidentally, you'd be surprised at the number of calls I've been getting from other advertising agencies. The hottest rumor on the street these days seems to be that I'm going to drop your shop and give our account to one of your competitors." Before Bonham could respond to that, Norris added quickly, "A couple of agencies right here in Chicago, in fact, indicated that I might find a change very advantageous. No, that isn't the word they used. What was it they said? Ah, yes. 'Rewarding.' They said I'd find a change very 'rewarding.'"

And so, listening to another replay of that telephone call as he stared out of his office on the twentieth floor, Gary Bonham didn't really see San Francisco. He didn't see the clock on the Ferry Building or the soaring angles of the Bay Bridge; he didn't see the gray Navy ships moored at Treasure Island or the white triangle of sail scooting over the bay.

What he saw was a threat, and he let his mind walk around it, worry at it, wonder whether to fight it. And how.

If he fought and lost, his company would lose a great deal of money. Or worse: if Chet Norris and his multi-million-dollar account walked out the door, Gary Bonham's advertising agency would probably go out of business.

AT THE SAME TIME, farther down the California coast, Hollywood actor Paul Taylor picked up the ringing telephone in his "ragtop Rolls," as he called his Rolls-Royce Corniche.

Stopped for the traffic signal at Hollywood and Vine, Taylor talked while he watched people cross the street and bump into each other gawking at his car. As often happened when Taylor and his car stopped, pedestrian traffic stacked up around the glistening convertible. Its burgundy finish seemed to shimmer, lustrous as silk. Its creamy leather upholstery looked almost liquid.

But the gawking eyes weren't only on the Rolls. Curled up beside Taylor was a twenty-year-old blonde, semi-wearing a see-through off-the-shoulder silk-and-lace teddy. Both girl and teddy looked very wrinkled, as though they'd been slept in. Or on. Or hadn't slept. She'd worn the same flesh-toned teddy to Taylor's apartment last night, another in a long line of "actresses" who never wondered why there was a "wardrobe audition" for a radio commercial.

Now, nestled against Taylor's forty-four-year-old side, the girl seemed to be dozing.

Taylor looked fit and fine, as always, ready for anything anywhere. In fact, he felt like his favorite description of himself. He'd overhead it in a studio one morning from a singer who thought her mike was off. Watching him stride in for a session, primed for action, she'd whispered to another singer standing beside her, "Look at Paul! He always looks like: 'Stick 'em up, world!'"

The signal changed and Taylor eased his car forward, slowly parting the crowd standing there in the middle of Hollywood Boulevard. Into the car phone he said, "Wait a second," then he waved the phone over his head at the crowd. "Call for Mr. Kissinger! Is there a Henry Kissinger in the bar?"

Hearing the noise, the girl sat up beside Taylor. She stretched. Two of her parts nearly fell out of her see-through off-the-shoulder silk-and-lace teddy. The crowd applauded as Taylor drove away.

At Argyll he turned right, found a parking spot midblock across from a small recording studio, and finished his phone conversation with his agent.

"He didn't flat-out *say* it," the agent said. "He never actually *said* the word 'money.' But that's what he's after, babe. He wants a kickback. I *know* it."

Taylor grinned into the phone. "You're shittin' me. My nice, big bakery client?"

"Your nice, big bakery client."

Taylor let out a one-bark laugh. "Hah!"

"Don't laugh. It's not unheard of for a client to come suckin' around for a payoff. Rare, but not unheard of."

"Well, it's a first for me, Morrie."

"Hey, for me, too, babe. But I tell you, the man is serious."

"And I'll tell *you* something: Fat—fucking—chance."

The blonde stirred and rested her right hand on Taylor's crotch. "Did you call me?"

"What a lovely thought, my dear," Taylor said to the blonde. Looking down at her gently moving fingers, he said into the phone, "Gotta run, Morrie, something's come up." He reached up and flipped the latch above the windshield, then shifted the phone and squeezed his hand along the blonde's rump and between the seats. He pushed the button marked HOOD, and as the convertible top began to close he finished his phone call. "But don't worry about the bread man, Morrie. I'll straighten him out when I see him in London."

AND ON THE same morning in Chicago, a couple of time zones later but still at the same time, two men slid into one of the scarlet banquettes at the Water Tower Inn for their monthly Friday lunch.

One of the men was Chet Norris, the new director of marketing at Thomas Baking Company, the second-largest baking company in the United States.

The other man was sales manager for a printing firm. From Maine to California, his company produced every bread wrapper, every label, every package, and every point-of-sale piece, sign and poster used by the Thomas Baking Company. To the sales manager, Chet Norris was a Very Important Customer.

The two men ordered drinks, vodka martini straight up for the sales manager, tomato juice for Norris. The waiter handed each man a menu. The sales manager held the large, folio-sized sheet of heavy paper with one hand, while with the other he pulled an envelope from his inside jacket pocket. Still looking at his menu, he silently reached out and placed the plain white envelope, thick with hundred-dollar bills, on the table in front of Norris.

At that moment, across the dining room, Deborah Thomas walked through the door. Norris glanced up, saw her, smiled, and waved his right hand, while his left hand slid the envelope smoothly off the table, out of sight. Still smiling, he growled at the sales manager. "Never, ever, let anyone see you do that. Especially her. *Never.* Or one of your competitors will be sitting in that seat so fast you'll think he stole your pants!"

Deb Thomas arrived at the table and Chet Norris stood, arms wide, smiling. "And here she is: My favorite advertising manager and my favorite lady."

IN MUSKET BEACH, Tony Pratt put the phone down after talking with Abe Arthur and stepped out to the front deck of the cabin, where Pat leaned against the railing. "You're smiling," she said. "Good news?"

"Some."

"We're still going to London, I hope."

"Oh, yes. But I'm smiling mostly because you look so nice standing there in the sun."

"Well, thank you," she said. "It's a beautiful day." The sunlight glittered in her salt-and-pepper hair as she looked around at the clear blue sky, at two white gulls sailing overhead, at the ocean and the few people walking the beach. "I love this part of the world. Especially on days like this." She paused. "Hard to believe we'll soon be on the other side of the globe." She turned her head and smiled at Tony. "Exciting, but hard to believe."

He stood beside her and leaned his elbows on the rail. She paused again. *"And..."*

A tone in her voice made Tony turn. He looked at Pat and saw her smile turn a trifle sarcastic. "'And' what?"

"My bottom-line brain can't understand why your client is paying for all of you people to go to London to record his commercials."

"Instead of doing them in L.A.?"

She nodded. "Or anywhere else in the U.S. Wouldn't it be cheaper?"

Tony shook his head. "They plan to use and re-use these spots for a long time. By recording the tracks in England, they won't have to pay residuals, so they'll save quite a few bucks."

"Enough to cover travel expenses for—how many?"

"Chet Norris and Deb Thomas and Gary Bonham were planning to go to England anyway, to check out the possibility of introducing their products over there. They've already scheduled meetings to talk with distributors. So, the only extra travel expense is for Paul Taylor and me."

Tony straightened and stretched. "Actually, recording the spots there gives them a little extra to talk about with those British distributors."

"Well, then," Pat said. "This little scheme isn't as off-the-wall as I'd thought."

He smiled, glancing at her out of the corner of his eye. "But it's still an off-the-wall group you're getting mixed up with."

"I think I can handle it."

"Even Paul Taylor?"

"For a trip to London, even Paul Taylor."

THREE

The Sunday Before the Monday

THE AIRPORT IN Portland, Oregon, is to London's
Heathrow Airport as bean soup is to bouillabaisse.
Bean soup and bouillabaisse are cooked in pots.
The Portland airport and Heathrow have air-
planes.

Portland International Airport is not much bigger than its name. It would fit inside Heathrow with
barely a bulge, runways included.

Like Portland itself, the airport is clean. People
walking through frequently describe it as tidy, almost cozy. It has a carpet on the floor. Not just in
front of the ticket counters and in the restaurants
and the shops: everywhere, all the way to the end of
the concourses.

And it never feels crowded, not even when it's
crowded.

When Tony and Pat boarded their flight to London, they were two of six million people passing
through Portland International Airport that year.
When they stepped off in England, they were two

of *thirty-nine* million passing through Heathrow in the same year.

Pat walked beside Tony into the endless flood of people in one of Heathrow's terminals. She cringed for her husband. Taking him to a shopping mall on Saturday was more trouble than taking the dog to the vet. "This," she said, "is madness."

People streamed, ran, and drifted around her— herds of saried Indians, droves of caftaned Arabs, schools of suited Japanese, flocks of dashikied Africans, and gaggles of open-throated Americans.

Like the Pratts, everyone else was puffy-eyed, sleepy, draped with briefcases, camera bags and luggage and, like Pat and Tony, most looked intense and confused. It was the same expression seen on the faces of army recruits milling around in bus stations searching for their sergeant, if only they knew what a sergeant was.

To clear customs, Tony and Pat discovered that they had to stand in line to find out whether they were standing in the right line. Looking through the glass wall of the customs section, Tony was startled to see a familiar face staring back at him from the other side of the glass. In the next room, Gary Bonham was going through customs, too.

After customs, finally, they pushed through the doors to look for a bus or taxi into London and discovered that being outside was no better than being inside. The crowd was just as crushing and the air was worse. Gasoline and diesel exhaust made the air so thick it was almost chewable.

Tony and Pat could hardly hear each other over the noise of taxis, limousines, buses, racketing baggage carts and shouting porters.

Pat tapped Tony's arm and pointed through the bluish haze. Above the crowd several rough, hand-lettered cardboard signs waggled around, held high by uniformed drivers trying to avoid getting shoved into the bumper-to-bumper traffic at their backs. One of the signs read MS. HEALEY. Another said MR. WAINRIGHT and a third said U.S.C. STUDENTS.

Then, to the left of the uniformed drivers, a gap opened in the crowd and through it came a blonde and a redhead in matching pink bikinis. Over their heads they waved thin wood poles and between the poles flapped a banner: CAR FOR PAUL TAYLOR, WORLD'S GREATEST LOVER.

As if in answer, a deep, ringing voice sang out over the noise. "Somebody call my name?" And behind a porter pushing a baggage cart to clear a path, Paul Taylor strutted out of the crowd with a beautiful flight attendant on each arm. They hovered over him, beaming down, attentive as sitters with a favorite but unpredictable child. Or he might have been Napoleon leading the way to dinner. Or, as he yelled when he saw Tony, "Hey! Pratt! How's it look? Like an old Mickey Rooney movie?"

And he was right. He could have been leading a scene from *Babes in Arms* or one of the other old films. The girls in bikinis carried their banner center-stage as if choreographed, replacing the flight attendants, who smiled and waved and pranced away through the crowd, after Taylor gave each a friendly rub on the rump.

Flanked by the two bikinis, Taylor's grizzled red ringlets fluttered between them at about breast height. He was almost five feet two inches tall. His legs, short and thin as baseball bats, somehow supported a head and trunk that might have been made for a man standing six-feet-four. His head was large and oval, his trunk wide and deep. Somewhere in that trunk and head were the mechanics and the skill to produce a voice that earned hundreds of thousands of dollars every year in recording studios in Hollywood, Chicago, New York and London.

Taylor's voice, unrecognized because of his versatility, was heard in a nearly endless round of radio and television commercials, animated cartoons, animated feature films and recorded books. He could hoot like a foghorn in an echo chamber or whimper like a terrified child, squeak like everybody's idea of a mouse or "Ho-Ho-Ho" like everybody's idea of Santa Claus. He had, and developed, the gift to imitate anything from a sea lion to John Wayne to Audrey Hepburn to a loaded eighteen-wheeler grinding up an eight-percent grade.

Paul Taylor's voice had made him a millionaire several times over. Nearly every person in that mob at Heathrow, regardless of their nationality, knew and loved the characters he played. They'd laughed at his cartoon voices over and over again. But nobody recognized him. He was just an odd-looking little guy surrounded by beautiful women, for some reason. Probably money.

Taylor waved and Tony, Pat and Bonham followed his impromptu parade to a London taxi that stood at the curb, its driver fighting off would-be passengers.

At first glance it appeared to be a normal London taxi, a stubby, rectangular black Vauxhall with yellow roof lights. But there were differences. "It's my car," Taylor told Tony. "I bought it through my British agent. But I had a few changes made."

One change was creating an oversize boot on the back for luggage. Normally, the luggage went inside in the large empty space to the driver's left. But in Taylor's taxi this space was taken by a chair, a large leather club chair on a swivel, where Taylor immediately installed himself with the red-haired bikini on his lap.

Spinning his chair to face the passengers in the back of his cab, Taylor grinned at the other British bikini settling onto Bonham's lap, then he looked at Tony and Pat. "Everybody here?"

"The only thing that's missing is the client," Tony said.

The grin disappeared from Taylor's face. "If 'the client' doesn't watch his mouth, he may *stay* missing," he said, and spun around to the front.

Another difference between Taylor's cab and an ordinary London taxi was the tape deck set into the dashboard beside a stack of eight pushbutton cassettes. Clinging to the spine of each cassette was a ragged strip of masking tape with a title scrawled in thick black marker pen: ELEPHANT. JET TAKEOFF. STAMPEDE. CAR CRASH. VERA. Another twenty or so tapes rattled around in a small plastic box suspended under the dash.

With the Americans, their luggage and the two British bikinis crowded into the cab, Taylor's driver began inching away from the terminal. The clot of cars, buses, vans and little intraterminal baggage trains was almost immobile.

His car had barely got moving when Taylor reached over to the tape deck.

He punched the button marked VERA.

A tape clicked into place.

A loudspeaker behind the car's grill, another of Taylor's changes in his private taxi, began to quiver. Through the speaker a huge music-hall orchestra blared out over Heathrow Airport. Violins swooped, trumpets soared, and at ear-popping volume in her shrill, heroic voice, Vera Lynn sang her anthem of World War Two.

"There'll always be an England—

Traffic stopped.

"And England shall be free—

People stared.

"If England means as much to you—

Backs straightened, upper lips stiffened.

"As England means to me."

Taxis, buses, baggage handlers, travelers from around the world stood frozen, except for a graying bobby who snapped off a salute that twanged his tall helmet at Taylor's car winding through the dead-stopped traffic and making for the motorway.

FOUR

The Sunday Evening Before the Monday—
London

TONY AND PAT unpacked in the practiced cadence of the forever-married, quietly gliding around each other from bed to closet to drawer with pants and jackets and dresses, drooping from hangers, or with their hands full of underwear, socks, pantyhose, shaving kit, and cosmetics from Tony's slowly deflating garment bag.

At home they'd happily crammed the lumpy gray bag with almost more than it could hold. "Looks like a hippo in distress," Pat had said. Now they emptied it in a tired silence. Besides the opening and closing of closets and dressers, the only sounds were high-pitched glissandos from the garment bag as they zipped the zippers open and closed.

When they'd finished unpacking, Pat shoved the limp, empty bag out of her way and plopped down on the bed to give their bed-and-breakfast bedroom a much more careful examination than her quick glance and nod when they were ushered in.

It was a large, cheerful room. The flowered wallpaper was clean and simple. The woodwork, painted a pale yellow, glistened with a hard high-gloss finish like baked enamel. It had a private bath, something of a rarity in their B-and-B experience.

And the location was good. In London's Knightsbridge area off Brompton Road, two blocks left of Harrod's and two blocks down, it was in easy walking distance of several bus stops and subway stations. "Not 'subway,'" she corrected herself. "The Underground. The Tube."

Tony noticed her inspection. "Satisfactory?"

"Oh, yes. I was just thinking that it's very convenient."

"Good."

"However."

"Yes?"

"I still can't believe that you told the travel agent to book us into a B-and-B instead of a hotel." Seated on the edge of the bed, she folded the garment bag in half, pushed it to the foot of the bed, and swung herself around, stretching out with her hands under her head.

"If I'd put us in a hotel, it would've had to be the same hotel where Norris and Bonham and the others are staying. And although I cheerfully work

with clients and actors, I cheerfully refuse to eat
and sleep with clients and actors.''

"You must have made a lot of friends with *that*
remark.'' She reached out and patted the empty
half of the bed.

"I didn't make *that* remark,'' Tony said. He went
around to the other side of the bed and stretched
out beside Pat, each on their back, hands under
head, looking up at the white plank ceiling. "I just
let them assume that poor freelance writers don't
stay in the same digs as rich clients and account executives and actors. Which is not too far from the
truth, till I get my latest overdue check from the
publisher.''

"But the trip is paid for.''

"*My* expenses are paid. Not yours.''

"Even so, I'm sure we could afford—''

"Yes, we could. But right now, while we're here
relaxing comfortably in our bed, the rest of our little group is probably all huddled together in the
hotel bar beginning a night of drinking too much
and pretending to enjoy each other's company.''

"Ah.''

"Furthermore: would you be as relaxed as this if
you were in the same hotel with Paul Taylor?''

Pat shook her head. "Good point. No.''

"That's what I thought. And that's another reason why we're here and they're there.''

"Thank you." She rolled onto her side, resting her head in the hollow of his left shoulder. "That guy gives me the jim-jams."

"Paul's all right," Tony said. He slid his left arm down along her side and his fingertips began to massage the small of her back. "In fact, I enjoy working with him because he's so damned good. And he's fun."

"'Fun'?" She shook her head. "Creepy."

Tony's other hand came around and caressed Pat's ear. He lifted her hair and rubbed the back of her neck. "He's okay. You just have to get past his physical appearance."

"His appearance doesn't bother me. It's his attitude. So aggressive. Almost mean."

"Maybe that has something to do with his appearance."

"Did you hear what he said in the car? At the airport? Sounded like a threat."

"Hmm." Tony rolled onto his side and kissed her ear.

"'Hmm,' yourself." After a minute or so she said, "And I'll bet you've already locked the door, haven't you?"

"Mm-hmm."

"You devil, you."

After another minute or so the garment bag rattled to the floor. Nobody noticed.

WHILE TONY AND PAT savored the privacy of their
B-and-B, the others in their group were, as Tony
had guessed, sitting around a low cocktail table in
the lobby bar of their hotel about half a mile away.

The two from California—actor Paul Taylor and
Gary Bonham, Account Supervisor and part-owner
of the advertising agency—were entertaining their
late-arriving clients from Chicago. More correctly,
it was Taylor who entertained Chet Norris, Marketing Director of the Thomas Baking Company,
and Deborah Thomas, the company's Advertising
Manager.

Taylor was telling inside stories about bloopers
and flubs in Hollywood recording studios, com-
plete with cartoon voices, impersonations and
sound effects. As he paid off each story, bursts of
laughter exploded over their little circle.

It wasn't long before other people around the
room began to leave their own tables and gather
round. Some even brought their drinks from the
bar. New arrivals coming in to register at the hotel
stopped on their way to the desk to find out what
was going on and then stayed to listen. The little
circle had grown into a ring three layers deep when
Deb Thomas wiped tears from her eyes and said,
"You're wearing me out. I've never laughed so
hard in my life." Then she stood. "But I've got to
get some rest. Busy day tomorrow."

Taylor hopped up. "Me, too, much as I hate to lose an audience." He gave the crowd his Groucho Marx look, tapped the ash off an imaginary cigar, and said, "I wish I could lose weight as fast as I lose an audience." The crowd groaned. "But I have to go, too."

The crowd groaned again and under the noise Norris jumped to his feet, grabbed Deb's elbow, and said, "But I have plans for dinner. I assumed—"

Quietly but firmly, Deb said, "*You* may have plans for dinner, Chet. This is the first *I've* heard about it." She paused. Pushing his hand away, she picked her purse up by the shoulder strap and looped it over her shoulder. She shifted her weight as if to leave but then paused and looked at Norris again. "I'm not sure why or when you started assuming things about me, but I know it's time to stop." She turned and walked away, smiling at the crowd as it parted to let her pass.

Bonham and Taylor, both standing now, had overheard her exchange with Norris. They glanced at each other, poker-faced, but Taylor's eyes were laughing at Norris's embarrassment. Bonham seemed almost guilty. He quickly glanced away as though he hadn't heard a word.

Taylor broke the silence. "Well, one more drink won't hurt."

The three men sat down again as the circle around them broke up, the people drifting back to the bar, to the reception desk, to wherever they'd been before.

After a couple of sips of his drink and some tense and ragged conversation, Paul Taylor mumbled something about needing to "rest his voice for tomorrow" and said goodnight.

Gary Bonham watched Taylor leave. "Good," he said, and leaned forward with his elbows on his knees, holding his drink with both hands. "This gives us a chance to talk."

"About what!" Norris almost snarled.

Bonham kept his eyes on his drink, never looking up. "About our last telephone conversation, Chet. About 'augmenting' your income, as you put it."

Norris fixed his cold eyes on Bonham. "You heard what I said. There's nothing to talk about." He put his glass down hard. "The hell with this." He got up and stomped away.

Bonham sat without moving, staring into his glass. Then he shrugged, raised the glass, and finished his drink without stopping. He set his glass down and picked up Norris's and drank it. He pushed himself to his feet, started to leave, stopped, picked up Taylor's glass and drained it, head tipped back, ice cubes and whiskey dribbling around the corners of his mouth and down his chin, then he staggered to the elevator.

NORRIS HAD BEEN furious with Deborah Thomas. In his hotel room he paced back and forth, swearing about what he called her "embarrassing display."

But slowly he controlled himself. After several minutes he went into the bathroom for a quick wash and shave. When he came out, he called Deb's room.

He sat in the leather wingback chair listening to the phone ring. Twenty times. He put it down, picked it up, dialed again, and let it ring another twenty rings.

He hung up, hesitated, then dialed Bonham's room. Another twenty rings got no response.

He dropped the phone back onto its cradle. "Sonofabitch!" he said to himself. "Bonham? Out with Deb? Trying to hang on to the account that way? Would he have the guts?" He snorted. "Not a chance."

Norris frowned at the phone. After a few moments he picked it up again, dialed, and ordered dinner.

He never considered calling Paul Taylor's room.

FIVE

The Sunday Before the Monday—
London (continued)

TAYLOR'S ROOM WAS actually a suite—bedroom, bath, sitting room—and that's where Deborah Thomas sat while the phone rang and rang in her own room.

Curled comfortably in a big leather club chair, she watched Taylor pour J&B Scotch into a tall glass at the compact little bar in the corner of the room. "Make it very pale. Mostly water, with lots of ice. The British don't seem to understand about ice."

Taylor nodded. "You've noticed that, too? You almost have to beg for ice in your drink. And when they finally deign to drop in one small piece, they look as though you'd just said something disgusting about the Queen."

He stirred the drinks and carried them across the room. "And something else you should know, since this is your first visit to England. The British don't understand about martinis, either. You may *say,* 'Martini,' but what they *hear* is 'vermouth'—martini and Rossi vermouth. And that's what you get: a glass of vermouth. Warm."

Deb laughed and took the glass Taylor held out. "Thanks for the tip. And the drink." She raised the glass in salute. "And for inviting me to dinner. I enjoy your company."

"And I enjoy yours—"

"Thank you again."

"—so I tried to think of something we could enjoy together." Taylor perched on the arm of the couch, one foot on the floor, the other swinging free. "And after your little run-in with your boss it occurred to me that you might appreciate a quiet, semi-secluded dinner from room service. And maybe somebody to talk to."

Deb made a sour face. "'My boss.'" Her face softened into a small smile. "Technically, I guess Chet Norris *is* my boss. At the moment. But my father *owns* this company and—"

"I wondered about that."

"—and someday I'll be where Dad is. So I'm going through the chairs, learning how the different departments operate. This year it's marketing and advertising. Chet is supposed to be showing me how that side of the business works." She paused and smiled again. "You've heard of 'Management by Objective?' I think I'm one of his 'Objectives.'"

Taylor put on an overdone leer. "Ah-ha! Moving in on the boss's daughter, eh?"

Deb didn't smile. "He has more than that in mind, if my hunch is right: *marry* the boss's daughter, who will someday *be* the boss."

"My, my," Taylor said. "Such a tangled web—"

He was interrupted by a knock at the door, and when he opened it, there stood a very large serving cart with their dinner under inverted bowls of shining stainless steel. A small white-haired waiter peeked around from behind the cart.

Taylor stepped aside. The little old waiter straightened his bony arms and scrawny body and pushed the heavy cart into the room. Deborah and Taylor watched him lean into it as if to keep it from driving him back downstairs to the kitchen.

The cart rolled slowly over the carpet, like a tumbrel to the gallows, seeming to pull the little waiter across the room. Silverware jingled, steel bowls rattled. Taylor looked as though he wanted to get behind the cart and push, but instead he went back to his perch on the couch.

The cart stopped at the small round table by the windows. As the waiter began unfolding a starched linen tablecloth, Taylor turned back to Deb Thomas. "So you think Chet Norris has plans to marry the boss—meaning you. I assumed he was already married.''

'''Was' is correct. For about two years. And from what I've seen, it's a wonder it lasted that long.'' She shook her head.

''Women?''

She looked at him sharply then looked away, as though changing her mind about what she wanted to say. ''Not women. Work. Chet Norris works. All the time. Seven days a week. He has to be in on everything, every detail.'' She nodded at Taylor. ''Believe it or not, he even gets involved in talent payments.''

Taylor muttered, ''So I've heard.''

''What?''

''Nothing. Tell me something. Why did you look at me with such a funny expression when I said something about Norris and 'women'?''

Deb shifted a little in her chair. ''Well,'' she said, and stopped. Her face turned pink and she smiled. ''Well,'' she said, ''I hear you've had *five* wives?''

One of the waiter's stainless steel bowls rattled against a dish.

Taylor shook his head. ''Four,'' he said to Deb. ''The newspapers always get that wrong. There were only four.''

''And are they wrong about the reason why your last wife left?''

"Oh, come on. That's just a rumor." Taylor reached for her glass. "Another drink while he's serving?"

"No, thank you." Deb pulled her glass away and grinned. "She found you in bed with a girls' softball team?"

A stainless steel bowl bonged on the carpet. The waiter picked it up. "*Terribly* sorry, sir."

"Not a whole *team*," Taylor said, sitting back on the couch. "It was only the infield."

Another bowl hit the carpet but this one bounced. Bong, bong. Like a muffled Big Ben.

"Two o'clock already?" Taylor looked at the waiter scuttling for the door.

"P'r'aps you and madam'd best serve yourselves, sir."

SO THEY DID. And through a quiet, comfortable meal—"Amazing, for two people together for the first time," she said at one point—Paul Taylor learned a little about Deborah Thomas and Deborah Thomas learned a lot about Paul Taylor.

That he'd been born with short, spindly legs and a normal trunk. That his father had tried to "correct" him, driving him into athletics and exercise. And by the time his Marine Corps father—

"Oh, dear," Deb said.

"Worse," Taylor told her, "a Marine Corps *fighter pilot*."

"Yes. That's worse."

"Describe the most insufferable person in the world."

"Go ahead."

"A Marine Corps fighter pilot from Texas who graduated from Yale."

—by the time Taylor's father finally accepted the fact that his son would never be "normal," young Paul had become a physical fitness fanatic.

Born with an outsize torso, he developed it into a broad, deep, muscular machine. And he developed his voice, too, expanding its range and flexibility with the same diligence.

During grade school in Georgia, where his family was stationed, he also made himself the class clown. "Deliberately," he said. "Maybe in self-defense. I don't know."

But after they were transferred to Camp Pendleton in southern California, Taylor turned into a champion. He won prizes in high school with his voice and his flair for speech and debate. In college he was the star of his radio and drama classes.

One of his professors arranged an audition for him at the Disney studios—"I killed 'em. Simple as that."—and while he was still in college he started doing cartoon voices for movies, television shows and commercials. By the time he graduated, Paul Taylor had built a national reputation as one of the most versatile, most reliable and most expensive voice talents in Hollywood.

Deborah Thomas turned slightly in her chair, uncrossing her knees, leaning toward the table a little. Her left hand idly traced one of the starched creases near the center of the tablecloth. "You also have a reputation for something else." She said it softly. An odd intimacy had begun sometime during dinner—filling a wine glass? pouring the coffee?—when their fingertips touched, carelessly at first, then longer, then lingering.

Taylor repeated the word. " 'Reputation.' " He frowned. "Women?"

She nodded and he shrugged a shoulder. "It's something that happens sometimes. Sometimes women look at me and want to take me home and put me on the mantel. Then, when I don't stay there, they seem very surprised."

There was a second or two of silence. "What about you?" he suddenly blurted.

Startled, she said, "What about me?"

"You're what, twenty-eight? Twenty-nine? And still not married?"

Deb shook her head. "Nope." She looked down into her coffee cup. "Close. Once. Close for a long time."

Taylor was quiet for a moment. "Still hurts?"

She looked up. "Just sorry for the time wasted."

Shoving his hands above his head, he let his voice boom. "How can it be? A girl like you!" When he lowered his arms, one hand touched hers on the tablecloth, one finger running slowly across her fingers.

She smiled, teasing, not moving away. "What about 'a girl like me'? What do you see?"

He rested his other elbow on the table, cupping his chin. "I see a girl with hair that's almost too black, almost too frizzy. I see a girl with a face that's almost too broad and a nose that's almost too big with almost too many freckles. I see a girl with eyes that are almost too big and a mouth that's almost too wide and a chin that's almost too pointed. But this girl fits everything together perfectly. I see a pretty woman."

Deb stared at him, her face suddenly blank.

He said, "More. A pretty woman who's intelligent and quick and fun and will someday make someone feel very happy and very lucky."

She looked down at his hand touching her fingers. "That's nice." Her voice was soft. She pulled her hand away for a moment and then, without raising her eyes, she turned his hand over, palm up, and laid her hand in his. "About these women who take you home and put you on the mantel?"

"I thought we were talking about you."

"We are." She smiled and looked straight into his eyes, her own eyes shining. "Surprise me."

SIX

The Monday — Morning

BY EIGHT-THIRTY on Monday morning Tony'd
wrapped up his music session in Studio One at
London Sound Recording. By nine o'clock one of
the junior engineers had already cleaned the studio. He'd propped rows of folding chairs against
the left wall and shoved microphone booms and
stands into a corner. He'd rolled up a couple of
hundred feet of electrical cable and hung the black
coils on hooks under the control room window.
He'd even swept the floor, taking away nearly every
trace of cigarette ashes, paper clips, rubberbands,
pencil stubs and the other flotsam that twenty-five
musicians and singers usually leave in their wake.

For an hour and a half they'd been working full
blast. Now, all that was left in the dark and silent
studio was the scent of smoke, warm bodies and
spent energy.

But on the other side of the control room window, where Tony and Eric played back the tape of
the session, light and energy burned. Music
screamed through the four-foot speakers hanging

high on the wall, so loud that some of the speaker cones actually quivered.

Tony stood under the speakers in the small room, eyes closed, head craned back, listening to the music tracks he'd just produced. From a row of track lights on the ceiling, hard light poured straight down on his upturned face drawing out the veins in his closed eyelids, glinting off the gray spreading through his brown hair.

Beside Tony in the pool of light, Eric the engineer sat hunched over his console. Eric's head bobbed with the beat of the music. His hands hovered along the bank of dials and switches, adjusting sound levels as the tape played back—a little more flute here, dump the bass there, goose the rhythm under the brass.

Suddenly Tony snapped his fingers. Eric wouldn't have heard it if Tony'd fired a cannon, but he saw the motion reflected in the big glass window between the control room and the dark studio. He flicked a hand at the off-button, and the sound stopped as suddenly as Tony'd snapped his fingers.

"Start the fade right there," Tony said. Eric nodded and made a note on his cue sheet. "Slowly," Tony added. "Don't just dump it. Take it down slowly, two to three seconds, then we'll cue the announcer. But don't lose the band. Hold it just under his voice so we can feel it push.''

"Right, and keep it under till—?''

"You'll hear the drum kick, same as in the first track. Then the band hits again, four bars, and ends with a big button.'' Tony sat down in one of the chairs lined up at the long table beside Eric's console. "Run it back a couple of turns and let it roll. You'll feel it.''

Eric tapped a button and at the other end of the console a big twenty-four-track tape machine responded. Gears clicked. Lights blinked. The fat silver reels zipped around backwards, letting out the garbled shriek of rewinding tape. He hit another button and the reels stopped. Another button. Click. Blink. The reels turned slowly forward and music roared out.

The track ran for a few seconds before Tony tapped Eric on the shoulder, but Eric was already nodding his head, pulling the volume down a little. He let it run, holding the level down till he heard the drum kick, then he pushed it back up again for the last four bars and a chord that almost peeled paint off the walls.

Over the fading echo Tony said, "Great band.''

Eric smiled. "Excellent players,'' he said with his broad British accent. "All excellent players.''

"And they really swing. Even though, like every musician in the world, I imagine, they hated the early morning call." Tony looked at his watch. "And speaking of morning calls, it's after nine. Our voice talent should be here by—"

The rest of his sentence disappeared, swallowed by a loud, screeching garble like the sound of tape rewinding at top speed. Surprised, Tony and Eric blinked at each other before both turned to check the tape machines. The big round reels, silent and still, stared back, but the mad gobbling sound went on, gradually slowing and modulating till it became an imitation of Tony's voice, a perfect echo of his last sentence. "And speaking of morning calls, it's after nine-thirty. Our voice talent should be here by—"

Tony and Eric looked across the control room and saw Paul Taylor leaning against the wall by the door, his arms folded across his chest. Taylor went on speaking, this time in his normal voice. "The call was for nine, I was here at nine. But I'm not surprised that you didn't hear me come in. You guys play that tape so loud I could commit a murder in here and you'd never know it."

Taylor shoved away from the wall. "Anyway, I'm here." He walked over to the console, holding his hand out to Eric. "I'm Paul Taylor, the 'voice talent' Tony was talking about. Where do you want me, in the studio or in the booth?''

"In the isolation booth, I believe," Eric answered, glancing at Tony.

Tony nodded. "Let's try it. If we don't like the sound, we'll move him out to the studio." Looking at Taylor, he said, "How're you feeling? You look terrific."

Taylor flung his arms wide and looked down at his white bucks, his white flannel pants and his navy blazer. "This old thing?" he said. He fingered the scarf around his neck. "Actually, if I felt any better, I'd get arrested." He glanced around the control room. "Where's your pretty wife?" he asked Tony, and then in deep, round tones that parodied the style of an oldtime ham, "Am I to anticipate no prettier sight than this foul pair I see before me?"

"Pat took the river tour to Hampton Court this morning. She'll be back this afternoon. But Deb Thomas'll be here."

"Ah," Taylor breathed. "'The more angel she'—"

Tony grinned. "With Norris, of course."

"—'and the blacker devil.'"

"Shakespeare this early in the morning is unusual."

"Shakespeare probably got up earlier than this."

"And we hope to see that play while we're here."

"*Othello?* Where?"

"Stratford."

Eric cleared his throat. "Sorry to interrupt, gentlemen, but our studio charges by the hour. And the meter runneth."

"You're right," Tony said, handing a set of scripts to Taylor. "Shakespeare comes later."

Taylor took the scripts and started for the door. "Okay, let's rehoice."

SEEN THROUGH THE control room's wide glass window, the isolation booth looked like a small room extruded from the left wall of a larger room, a little studio inside a big studio. They were common in studios as old as London Sound.

Originally, they separated the sound sources, preventing an actor's microphone from picking up other sounds—music from the orchestra, for example, or a sound effect. By isolating the sound sources, the theory was, technicians in the control room could get a better balance between voice, music and sounds.

As microphones and recording techniques improved, the isolation booth became unnecessary. But if a studio had one, Tony liked to use it, as he explained a few minutes later to Deb Thomas. "If we were recording Paul and the band live, we'd put him in the booth. With his mike isolated like that, his voice track would be clean and we wouldn't hear any music in the background. So if, later, we decided to edit or cut his voice tape, there wouldn't be any music behind him to go out of sync where we spliced the tape.'' He looked at Deb to make sure he'd explained himself clearly. "Okay?"

Deb nodded.

She and Gary Bonham had arrived just after Paul had gone into the studio. Chet Norris had walked in a couple of minutes later. Seeing Deb and Bonham together, he'd stopped, frozen. "Didn't you two get enough of each other last night?" Deb and Bonham had looked at each other and shrugged.

Now, Bonham stood in a corner. Norris paced, tense and nervous, as Deb asked Tony, "But this music track is already recorded. We're just over-dubbing Paul's voice. Why put him in the booth?"

"Because I think it gives his voice more 'presence.' Gives it a more 'intimate' sound. Gets the listener a little more involved."

"Alright, alright," Norris growled. "Cut the pontificating and get on with it."

Ignoring Norris's remark, Tony smiled at Deb to encourage any other questions she might have. But at the same time he leaned toward the talk-back mike wired to a speaker in the studio. He clicked the switch and looked in at Taylor. "Ready, Paul?"

"Paul ready," he answered.

"Cute," Norris sneered.

Argumentative, unpleasant, negative, carping. Those were the kindest thoughts Tony had about Chet Norris during the next thirty minutes. At one point Eric tilted his head toward Tony and muttered, with fine British understatement, "Is your client wound a trifle tight this morning?"

The music was terrible, Norris complained. The band played out of tune. The arrangements were amateurish.

And then Paul Taylor started reading the copy. Before he'd finished his first take, Norris interrupted. "Tell him to do it again."

Taylor started another take. Then, phrase by phrase and sentence by sentence, Norris began correcting the reading of a man who earned almost a million dollars a year with his ability to read.

Taylor showed remarkable restraint. Each time Norris gave him a new interpretation, he echoed it precisely. Every word that Norris wanted emphasized, Taylor emphasized. Every inflection that Norris wanted changed, Taylor changed. Every pause that Norris wanted, Taylor gave him to the millisecond.

Deb didn't look at him. She watched Norris, almost hypnotized.

Tony restrained himself, too. He assumed that Gary Bonham, as the agency representative and account supervisor, would soon exert some diplomatic control over his client. But after Norris's seventh or eighth interruption Tony noisily pushed back his chair and stood up. Chin raised, he stared at Bonham as if to say, "Well? Do something about your client."

Bonham opened his mouth but Norris interrupted. "Gary Bonham doesn't have anything to say." He smiled at his agency man. "He knows what it takes to keep our business."

Deborah Thomas looked from Norris to Bonham and back, speechless, as if wondering whether she'd heard what she thought she'd heard.

Bonham's face didn't change. It stayed blank and cold. But his bloodshot eyes stared back at his client, hard.

Tony broke the silence. He flipped the talk-back switch and said, "Let's take about five, Paul. Okay?"

"Okay." Taylor hopped off the tall stool he was using and yanked off his blazer. "But first let me do it one more time, straight through. Music cued up?"

Tony looked at Eric, Eric nodded, and the tape reels turned. "Here it comes," Tony said. The music track played, in the control room and in Taylor's headset. Following Tony's cues in and out of the music, Taylor read the copy without interruption exactly as he'd read it on the first take.

The music track ended and Norris stood up, smiling. "Perfect," he said, "just the way I told him. Now why couldn't he do that earlier?"

Tony leaned over the talk-back and said, "That's a keeper, Paul. Let's take a break." Before Taylor could say anything, Tony added, "I'll bring you some coffee and we can talk in there about the other tracks."

IN THE CORRIDOR behind the control room, Bonham said he "wanted to get some air" and walked away, leaving Deb and Norris standing at the entrance to the clients' lounge. Norris looked at Deb. "Aren't you going with him?"

"Why?"

"After last night?"

"What are you talking about? That's the second time you've said something about 'last night.'"

"I called you. For dinner."

"I went out."

"Then I called Gary's room."

"So?"

"He was out, too."

"So?"

"So naturally I assumed that you—"

"I told you, Chet: you assume too much about me. And what was that remark you made in the control room about Gary? 'He knows what it takes to keep our business.'"

"Private joke between Gary and me. Want some tea?"

"Sounded like a threat. No. No tea. I'm going back inside with Paul and Tony. Dad sent me with you to learn, you know." She turned away and then stopped, looking at him over a shoulder. "I wonder if I'm learning more than I bargained for. And I wonder if my father knows how you handle the people you do business with."

Going back into the control room, Deb found nothing but its constant electrical hum and the residual odor of several nervous bodies confined in a small, warm space. She looked through the window into the studio and saw Tony, Eric and Paul talking very seriously.

She hesitated and then, deciding, she went back to the corridor and pushed open the heavy door into the studio. As she walked in she heard Eric say, "...a little studio time open tonight, if we don't finish this morning. But except for an hour tomorrow afternoon, the studio's booked all the rest of the week."

Tony said, "So tonight's the best bet." Eric nodded and Tony asked Taylor, "Can you come back tonight, if necessary?"

Taylor looked at Deb as she came toward him. He winked at her and said, "Sure. I'd walk a mile for a Thomas."

Deb stopped beside Taylor and out of the tail of his eye Tony saw her hand wrap around Taylor's and then quickly let go. He looked at them and they looked back, straight-faced, standing so close together that their bare arms grazed each other.

Equally straight-faced, Tony said, "Do I see before me the source of our Mr. Norris's irritation?"

Deb shook her head, once. "He doesn't have a clue."

"Can we keep it that way? Till we get these spots done?"

"Why should we." The way Taylor said it, it wasn't a question.

Tony answered it anyway. "To keep Norris from being more of a problem than he is already. Especially for Deb."

Taylor looked at Deb. "Think so?" he asked with a grin. "Considering your position in relationship with management?"

She wrinkled her nose and nodded once. "Maybe a little."

He turned back to Tony. "You got it."

face, Taylor said, quietly again, "I have a reputation in this business for doing a job right and doing it fast."

Norris began to push himself up from his chair at the table. "I don't have to—"

"Shut up!" Taylor's growling roar shoved Norris back into his chair and Taylor went on smoothly, explaining. "On ninety percent of my dates, I walk into a studio and record a piece of copy in one take. On a bad day I may have to go two takes. Three at the most."

Norris swivelled his chair and put his back to Taylor, starting to get up. "You little freak, you'll never work for—"

Taylor's big hands thudded down on Norris's shoulders and his thumbs bored into the muscles below his neck. "Siddown!" Norris sat, holding his back stiff and straight trying to relieve the pain. Taylor spun Norris around in the chair to face him again.

The actor pitched his voice low and quiet. "I'm proud to be one of the few people in L.A. who can walk into a studio and deliver like *that*." He snapped a finger. "There's me, there's Ed McMahon, maybe one or two more. I'm very proud of that." He paused but no one moved. The steady electric drone seemed to hold every person in place, hypnotically. Motionless, each one listened to Taylor. But they all watched Norris trying to flex his shoulders, flinching at the pain and then falling back as Taylor yelled, "But now what! We've been here for an hour-and-a-half and we've got one spot done? And five more to go? And you've got things so screwed up you'll be lucky if you walk out of here with *anything!*"

Taylor turned to leave, then spun back. "In fact, you'll be lucky if *you* walk out of here!"

He turned and swung back once more and this time his voice was very quiet. "And what's this shit about 'never working for you again'? I've already *decided* that. I decided *that* as soon as my agent told me about the little scam you tried to pull. I'd never have kept *this* date if it hadn't been for two things. One, I'd promised Tony Pratt. Two, the free trip. So. Now who's the 'freak,' you freaky sonofabitch?"

This time when Taylor turned, he kept going, down the stairs and out the door, shouting over his shoulder, "Hotel, Tony! In the bar!"

For a few seconds, the only sound in the room was the low-pitched hum. Then Norris stood, flexing his shoulders. Bonham coughed and said, "Well—" and Tony said, "Right. Let's pack it in for the day and come back tomorrow for that hour of studio time that Eric has opened and—"

"No," Norris said. Slowly he walked around to the other side of the console. He stood in the shadows, his back to the studio window, and said it again, shouted it. "No! You finish today!" He raised his right arm, wincing at the pain in his shoulder, jabbing a finger at Tony. "You get that goddamned little prima donna back in here and finish your job today or Thomas Baking is *not* paying for it."

For the first time, Gary Bonham spoke up. "Wait a minute, Chet—"

"'Wait a minute' your ass. Your agency made the schedule. We agreed to it. Anything beyond that is the agency's responsibility. Understand that, Gary? It means *you pay!* Studio time, musician's time, the whole thing, including talent fees." He paused and sneered. "*Talent.*"

Deborah Thomas moved into the chair Norris had left and said, "Chet, don't you think—"

"Please, Deb. Don't interfere. You said you were here to learn, so listen and learn how to keep these people in line. They've got to be reminded that this account is *not* a money tree." With barely a breath Norris turned on Bonham again. "Did you hear me, Gary? If this job isn't finished today, *the agency pays.*" He smiled a grim smile and added, "That'll be *another* bill coming due for you."

Gary Bonham's only response was to stiffen against the wall, and his angry expression melted into the same sightless mask he'd worn in his office while he listened to Norris's threatening telephone call.

But Deb and Tony both started talking at once. Norris raised his hands, shaking his head. Deb stopped but Tony kept talking. " . . . finish later today. We've almost run out of time and there's another session booked right behind us."

Norris continued shaking his head as Tony persisted. "Eric says there's some time open this evening. We'll come back and make a fresh start—"

"No!" Norris almost screamed it. His face paled and his voice shook. "I said no! And stop trying to weasel your way out of this, Pratt. Get the job done or—"

"That's what I'm trying to do, Chet, if we can start fresh tonight—"

"I'm through talking to you, Pratt. In fact, I'm through with you, period. The woods are full of so-called 'producers' who'd *pay* to work on this account. So get this job done, because it's the last job you'll ever have with this company."

"Chet!" Deb said. "You can't do that!"

"And when I get back home, I plan to get on the phone to tell every client I know just how incompetent and unreliable you really are."

Deb suddenly slammed her hand down on the table. "Listen to me, Chet!"

"Stay out of this, Deb."

"You're being ridiculous."

"You don't know anything about it."

"I know enough to stick with people who've worked for us for years, who've helped us get where we are."

"Doesn't mean a thing."

"It does to me. And as advertising manager, this is my responsibility now, not yours."

"What!"

"Not any more. It's *my* job." She turned to Tony. "And if you can get it done tonight, do it."

Tony looked down at Eric, still sitting quietly at his console. "Eric?"

"Six o'clock. The receptionist leaves at five and locks the front door, but I'll get you a key. You can let the others in."

Tony turned to Chet. Norris ignored him, looking at Deb. "I have theater tickets for tonight. For you and me."

"I'll be here."

Norris took a deep breath. He clenched his teeth. Muscles rolled under the tight skin of his jaws. He blew the breath out and said in a thin, tense voice, "All right. Forget that. But you may remember the marketing department's presentation to your father—that we have better reasons for coming to England than to save a few dollars on this lousy recording session."

Deb started to say something but Norris's voice rose and cut her off. "If the Thomas Baking Company is going to penetrate this market by next year, the time to move is now. According to plan. Tomorrow and the rest of the week we've got appointments to keep, distributors to see in Leeds and Manchester and Birmingham. We've got to move on and not waste any more time with these people. This job has to be finished today."

He paused for a breath and Deb cut in. "It *will* be finished. Today. This evening. I'll handle it myself."

Norris stood behind one of the wooden swivel chairs lined up around the table. He grabbed the chair back and leaned forward, arms straight down and stiff, gripping the chair so hard that his tan fingertips turned white. "Okay, Deb. I hope you won't be sorry," he said, his voice still thin and quiet.

He shifted his grip and suddenly the chair went crashing into the wall under the window. Chunks of pale plaster exploded. The back of the chair shattered and one of its casters flew loose and skidded clattering across the floor till it stopped with a tinny thump against one of the tape machines.

The racket died, leaving that familiar electric hum. In the quiet Norris said, "But you're going to have one hell of a time getting this stuff approved by the marketing department." He stomped across the room, down to the door, and out.

The heavy door sighed shut. Eric breathed an echoing sigh. He leaned back in his chair. "Well, some of *that* was plain enough." He flipped a ragged dustcloth across the dials and knobs of his console. "P'r'aps we're beginning to break the Americans' code."

SEVEN

The Monday—London

DEBORAH THOMAS perched on the edge of the green wicker love seat in the clients' lounge. "I won't say I'm not nervous about it, but I'm not backing down."

She paused to sip tea from a white crockery mug. Tony Pratt and Gary Bonham stood across from her by a big red Coke machine. Tony had a Coke can in one hand. Bonham clutched a tall glass of Scotch and water. "Mostly Scotch," he'd said when Eric offered drinks after their explosive morning.

Deb looked up at Tony over the rim of her mug. "So call Paul and let him know we're on—" She interrupted herself to set the mug on the wicker arm and reach for her purse. "No. I'll call him myself. Either of you happen to have the hotel phone number?"

Tony snapped his briefcase open to look for his notebook.

Bonham gulped from his glass. "Before you do that, Deb, there's something I'd like to talk to you about."

"About the session?"

"No. About Chet."

She pulled an envelope from her purse. "Ah. Here it is, on the itinerary. Never mind," she said to Tony, "I found the number." Then she looked at Bonham as she stood and started for the telephone on a table in the corner. "First, let's make sure we find Paul and get him lined up for tonight. Okay, Gary?"

Bonham gulped again. "Whatever you say. But I think it's something you and your dad should hear. Especially J.T."

"Her father's in Chicago," Tony said. "How would he hear any—"

Deb spun the telephone dial, and over the ratcheting noise she said loudly, "I'd rather wait, Gary. I really would. Let's talk about it after the session tonight."

FORTY-FIVE MINUTES LATER, in a handsomely understated restaurant in London's Belgravia section, she sat smiling across a small round table at Paul Taylor as he finished boning her Dover sole. "I'm glad you suggested lunch."

"I'm glad it was you who called. Otherwise I might be doing this for Pratt or Bonham." He handed the plate across to Deb.

"And I'm impressed that you were able to reserve a table and order lunch. On very short notice."

"Restaurants are easy to handle, if you speak their language." Taylor shrugged and worked the knife neatly through his own serving of sole. He transferred the skeleton to another plate and watched as a waiter quickly took the bones away. "Beverly Hills or Belgravia, they're much the same."

"That may be so. Still, I'm impressed."

"Good. It's part of my plan. Wine?"

Nodding, she said, "Which is?"

"For us to spend a great deal of time together."

"Good plan." She raised her glass and tasted. "Mm. And good wine, too. French?"

"American."

"Ah. I should have guessed. Knowing your California roots, this must be a California wine."

Taylor shook his head. "Oregon."

Raising her glass for another sip, she stopped, surprised. "Oregon? Wine?"

"Some very fine wines are coming out of Oregon these days."

Deb tasted it again. "What a surprise. But how'd it get here?"

"I sent it. A case. Two weeks ago."

She shook her head and smiled. "Now that's *very* impressive."

"I repeat, it's part of my plan. Eat, before your fish gets cold."

"Yes, sir. Tell me more about your plan."

"To see as much of you as I can."

Her face turned pink around a small smile and she said, "You saw quite a bit of me last night." She put her knife and fork on her plate.

"And very nice it was."

"Very, very nice."

He reached across the table and held her hand. "I can see us doing more of that."

"Yes."

"And more *than* that."

"Yes."

He picked up his glass of wine. "Oregon, for example. I'd like to show you my place on the Oregon coast."

She gripped his hand but the smile left her face. "That's a problem, isn't it?"

"What?"

"Oregon. California." She shrugged. "You live on the West Coast. I live in Chicago."

With a laugh he said, "And now we're in London. A few thousand miles every couple of weeks is no big deal any more, thanks to the miracle of flight." His voice was suddenly a deep, comic caricature. "Great silver bird fly everywhere. Even Or-ree-gawn. No more stagecoach. Stagecoach gone two, maybe three weeks now."

The corners of Deb's mouth moved, a sorry little smile as she stared at him. In those few seconds Taylor saw her bright eyes dim, saw the light far behind them flicker like a candle at the end of a long hall.

She looked away, and when she looked back, the glitter in her eyes was tears. Her voice came out low and matter-of-fact. "I guess I'm making a fool of myself," she said. "You're not thinking about something like, 'I can see us being together for a long, long time.' What you're thinking about is, 'Next time you're in town, Deb, let's get together.' Right?"

"No, that's not what I'm thinking, not at all. I—"

She pulled her hand away from his, shaking her head. "I can't believe I'm saying these things, feeling these things. And I know a one-night stand is no basis for—"

"You know it's more than that."

"What?"

"We *both* know it's more than that."

"What, then? Tell me."

Taylor leaned forward, reaching for her hand. He opened his mouth and the waiter said, "Everything satisfactory, sir? Shall I remove these plates?"

"What? No. Yes, take them away." Taylor flapped his hand over the table and sat back, muttering. "How can I expose myself over a plate of cold fish?"

"Sir?"

"Go ahead." He looked at Deb. "And coffee." She shook her head. "Tea." She nodded. "And a pot of tea, please. Just bring it and leave it. And the check, please. Thank you. Stop. Leave the salad. She didn't eat the fish, so leave the salad. And the bread and butter. Thank you. And notice the large electric sign above this table. 'Do Not Interrupt Or We'll Take You To The Tower And Lose The Key.'"

"Yes, sir."

As the waiter walked away, Taylor did his Groucho Marx impression for Deb. "'Yes, sir'? What do you suppose he meant by *that*?"

Deb watched his performance with serious eyes and not a trace of a smile. "You were about to tell me something," she said. "Tell me. This is not time for clowning."

Taylor frowned, watching his hand brush a few crumbs off the table top. "As Dr. Johnson said, 'I live in the world of jollity not so much to enjoy company as to shun myself.''' He gulped some wine and put the glass down far to the side, as if dismissing it, before he laced his fingers together and leaned forward, seeming to gather himself, preparing for something he wasn't sure of.

Once more he looked across the table at Deborah Thomas, at her hair, her lips, and then straight into her eyes. "Last night you heard more about me than most people learn in a lifetime. I told you things that I thought I would never tell anyone again. You and I talked to each other in a way that I didn't really believe was possible."

He took a deep breath, and as he let it out, he said, "For some reason we made a kind of—I don't know how to describe it. It's very rare. We flew halfway around the world, separately, apart. And here, suddenly, two separate people made a 'connection' of some kind. All of a sudden I feel closer to you than—I can't describe it. I don't have the words for it and I thought I had the words for everything." Deb reached across the table and slipped her hand between his. "It's wonderful. It is. Full of wonder."

She nodded, eyes brimming, as he unlocked his fingers and held her hand between his.

"But!" he said. He frowned and quietly bumped their hands on the tabletop.

Half smiling, she said, "But what?"

"But then I remember what I am."

"What you are is very, very different from the kind of man I meet."

"That's true."

"I wish I'd met someone like you a long time ago."

"They didn't make many like me."

"*That's* true."

Taylor frowned and shook his head. "You saw me."

"I certainly did." She smiled and squeezed his hand.

He jerked away, leaving her hand empty on the stark white cloth. "Right," he said, reaching for his glass. He filled his mouth with wine and gulped it down.

"Paul—"

"Facts, Deborah." He put the glass down. Sitting straight in his chair, he stretched his arms and grabbed the edges of the table. "Think of what I'm like below this table."

"Paul—"

"If I stood up right now, I wouldn't be much taller than I am sitting down. In bed I can be seven feet tall. But when morning comes, I'm back to normal. Which is abnormal. Think about that. Not. Normal. And I won't let you commit yourself to that."

"Paul, don't you think that I understand—"

"No. Right now you're very susceptible. Whether you realize it or not, you're still in mourning for your near-miss marriage. You told me that last night. I don't want to cause you any more hurt. And I know—I *know*—that someday you'll look at me and remember what Chet Norris called me this morning." Taylor let out a snort. "It's the only time he was right."

"What?"

"You'll look at me and think, 'What am I doing with this little freak?' "

Deb slapped the table with both hands. "That's ridiculous!"

"It's a fact. You'll think it and I'll see it in your eyes. 'What am I doing with this little freak?' And you'll hate yourself for thinking it and you'll hate me for knowing." He paused, then quietly said, "And I don't want you—or me—to go through that."

There was a long silence, Deb staring down at the top of the table, Paul watching her.

She sat back in her chair, then, and looked at him sitting across from her, tense and stern. When she began to speak her voice was low and her pace was slow, but her pace picked up as she spoke. "One of the appealing things about you is your concern for me. Which came through even then, in what you just said. And it must have taken a lot of guts to say those things about yourself. Ridiculous as they are, it must have taken a lot of guts to say them.'' Taylor opened his mouth but she kept talking. ''And now that you've said them, I'm about to dump this salad over your stupid head. And don't ever think such thoughts again because, if you do, I'll see it in your eyes and I'll *know* and I'll dump *another* salad over your stupid head. And I'll follow you, across London, across California, through the wilds of O-ree-gawn, following the trail of salad dressing dripping off your stupid head. Now drink your wine, pay the check, and let's go.''

She stood, bumping her chair backwards with the backs of her legs, and stomped away.

TAYLOR DROVE DEB to their hotel in his modified London Cab. It was a short, silent ride. Seated behind the steering wheel, he tried to pick up the conversation where Deb had stopped it, but she raised a hand and said, ''All I want to hear from you is one of two things. One is 'I'll never talk that way again.' The other is 'Here's the hotel, watch your step, I'll call you when it's time to leave for the studio.' ''

So they rode through London in silence—or, as silent as London can be in midafternoon—with Taylor at the wheel, alternately frowning and smiling, and Deb in the swivel chair beside him, spinning right and left, looking at the sights.

When they drove up the curving driveway at the hotel entrance and the doorman opened the passenger door for Deb, Taylor said, "Here's the hotel, watch your step, I'll call you when it's time to leave for the studio."

Deb stepped down, turned, and asked, "What time, do you think?"

Taylor shook his head and pointed to his compressed lips.

She nodded. "Dispensation. You may answer."

"Five-thirty," he said. "Would you like to—"

A warning finger shot up and she said, "Ah-ah! One answer! No questions. Five-thirty. I'll be ready." She turned and strutted away like a proud thoroughbred, head high and tail swinging.

Taylor grinned and watched her march through the gleaming glass doors before he let his car roll to a stop beside the no-parking sign at the end of the driveway arc. Walking back to the entrance, he folded a five-pound note around his car keys. The doorman opened the door with his right hand and Taylor dropped the bill and keys into his left. "Thank you, sir. I'll 'ave 'er ready. Five-thirty."

Crossing the lobby on his way to the bank of elevators, Taylor passed the entrance to the bar just as Gary Bonham rushed out. The five-plus Taylor ricocheted off the six-plus Bonham with a thump and an "Oomf" and Bonham caught Taylor in midair, grabbing him by the shoulders before his feet touched the floor.

"I'm terribly sorry, sir," Bonham croaked in a cloud of Scotch fumes. "Jeez. I beg your—Oh, Paul."

Taylor tugged and brushed at his clothes, trying to recover a little dignity. "What the hell's going on, Gary?"

Again, Bonham's words stumbled out in another fog of Scotch, as though the hot whiskey fumes had melted the words and fused them together. "Thought I saw. Saw Deb. Saw Deb Thomas?" Bonham's bloodshot eyes peered anxiously over the lobby. He looked slightly frantic, with his silver-tipped hair dangling down his forehead. He made it worse by scrubbing his knuckles through it again.

"What? Say it once more, one word at a time."

"Deb Thomas. Thought I saw her. Go through the lobby. Past the bar."

Taylor patted Bonham's arm and began steering him toward one of the tables along the wall. With his free hand, Taylor waved for one of the waiters to bring coffee. "That's right. You did see her. Or, at least, she went by here."

"Good. Good. Got to talk to Deb."

"She's gone upstairs to rest. I think you should do the same. I mean, sit over here and have a little rest." Bonham slumped into a chair and Taylor sat down across the table from him. "Have a couple of belts did you, Gary?"

"Sev'ral. How 'bout another, where's the waiter?"

"He's on the way. I thought you and booze weren't speaking any more."

"Me, too. Guess not. Jeez. One's too many and a hundred's not enough." He wagged his head. "Goddammed Norris. Sometimes I hate this fucking business."

"Hey. Watch your language," Taylor said, half-smiling. "You're in a classy joint."

"And I'm a classy guy. You're a classy guy. Everybody's classy but Chet Norris. That goddammed Chet Norris. Never had a client like him. Crooked sonofabitch. Reminds me. Got to see Deb. Where is she? What's that?" He stared down at his cup as the waiter filled it with steaming coffee.

"Coffee," Taylor said. "Have a little coffee."

"I don't want coffee. Got to see Deb."

"She's in her room. Resting. So let's let her rest. You can tell me all about it while we have some coffee. Drink."

Obediently, Bonham picked up the cup. "Don't want any coffee. Got to tell *Deb*. Something she oughta hear." He held the delicate china cup in both hands and sipped coffee, spilling no more than a fourth of it before he put the cup down on the tablecloth. "Got something her *old man* oughta hear."

"Something to hear? Have some coffee." Taylor poured from the silver pot into Bonham's cup.

Again Bonham hoisted his cup and swallowed. "Evidence." He swallowed more coffee. "Not evidence. Proof! That crooked sonofabitch," he muttered again. He gulped once more and suddenly put the cup down. "Proof! Reminds me, let's have a drink. I don't want this crap."

Taylor poured more coffee. "We'll have a drink later," he said. "After the session I'll buy drinks all night. Tell me about your 'evidence' and why you want to give it to Deb. Have some coffee. Cheers." He raised his cup and Bonham dutifully raised his. Taylor sipped. Bonham gulped. Then Taylor said again, "Why do you want Deb to have this 'evidence,' whatever it is?"

"So she can take it to her old man. Play it for her old man. Let old man Thomas hear what a crook he's got workin' for him."

"'Play it?—let him hear it'? You mean you've got Norris on tape? Doing something crooked?"

Bonham nodded and didn't stop. "Got him." He kept nodding. "Good old Chester P. Norris on the telephone. On tape. Right here." Still nodding, he tapped his sports jacket on the left side and Taylor heard an audio cassette rattle in its plastic case. "Right here in the pocket over my heart, that's where I've got the sonofabitch. Tryin' to shake me down." His head continued bobbing up and down, like a broken toy.

"Stop," Taylor said. "Stop doing that." Reaching across the table, he grabbed Bonham's head and held it with one hand while he poured more coffee with the other. "Hold still or your head'll snap off and roll across the floor and trip somebody."

Bonham blinked and looked around the floor. "Where?"

"Terrible scene. Drink your coffee."

"I want a Scotch."

"Screw the Scotch. Drink the coffee. D'you mean you've got Chet Norris on tape telling you, the agency, to pay him, the client, money?"

"Correct."

"Or else he'll take his account to another agency?"

"Correct."

"He wants a kickback?"

"You got it, pal."

"Well, I'll be damned," Taylor said, remembering his own conversation on the car phone when his agent Morrie told him that Norris was hinting at a kickback. "But why get Deb involved? Go straight to her old man. Or the cops. Don't get Deb involved."

A puzzled look spread over Bonham's face. For several moments he squinted silently across the table at Taylor. "What's wrong with this picture?" he mumbled quietly to himself. He sipped some coffee, waiting for an answer. When he didn't get one, he gave up and answered Taylor's questions. "Cops'd take too long. Give the tape to Deb, let her play it for the old man, get rid of the sonofabitch Norris *right now*." He tried to snap his fingers but they didn't work. "Anyway, that's what I want to do. Get the sonofabitch gone."

"So what's Deb gonna do? Play the tape over the phone to her father?"

"Right."

"Does she carry a cassette player around?"

"Maybe."

"Do you?"

"Of course not."

"Of course not. And even if you did, the playback from one of those things wouldn't be clear enough for a trans-Atlantic call."

"Why not?"

"Come on, Gary, turn your lights on!"

Bonham poured coffee for himself. "I'm beginning to see what's wrong with this picture." He put the pot down and looked at Taylor. "Go on."

"You taped a telephone call, or calls, from Norris, right? Probably on a little mickey-mouse recorder you picked up in a discount store. Right?"

"Go on."

"So the sound's probably a little muddy to begin with—a little hard to understand. So now you want to play it back? Through that mickey-mouse cassette player? Into another telephone? And hope that somebody listening on the other side of the ocean can understand it?"

"No?"

"No way. But I think I know how to do it. We'll have to go back to the studio to check it out, listen to the tape, and set it up. And if it works, I'll even pay for the phone call."

"How come?"

"Because the bastard tried to pull the same scam on me."

"No shit."

"No shit." Taylor looked at his watch. "Four-thirty. I wonder if the studio's open."

"We can get in. Tony gave me a key."

"That's not what I mean. I wonder if the other session is finished, so we can use the control room. We'll have Eric set up the tape, run it through the board and clean up the sound as much as he can, and then patch it into the phone line." Taylor looked at his watch again. "If we're lucky, you can catch old man Thomas in Chicago before he goes to lunch."

"I'd rather have Deb call him," Bonham said.

"Bullshit!" Taylor leaned across the table and said in a cold, hard voice, "I told you. Keep her out of it. Norris can be a mean bastard. You remember how he was this morning. I don't want her exposed to any of his shit. Is that clear to you, Gary?"

"Okay. All right. I'll do it."

"Good." Taylor waved to the waiter and signaled for the check. "Let's go."

As they pushed their chairs back and stood, Bonham said, "I want to stop in the men's room first. All that coffee."

"Sure. Coffee." Taylor's voice had a little laugh in it. "Scotch is a solid, right?"

Bonham's eyes narrowed and he looked down at Taylor. "Meet you outside," he said, and walked away to the men's room.

Taylor signed the check, went out the front door and waited while the doorman brought his taxi around and held the driver's door open for him.

Settling behind the wheel, Taylor turned and looked back at the entrance. A couple came out just then, and through the open door behind them Taylor could see across the hotel lobby, where Gary Bonham was replacing the receiver of one of the house telephones.

Silently Taylor watched Bonham walk out of the hotel and around the front of the car and climb into the passenger seat. Silently he steered his cab out into the London traffic for the short drive to the recording studio. Quietly, glancing at Bonham, he said, "You look better. Feel better?"

Bonham nodded. "Head's clearer."

"Good. Who were you talking to on the phone?"

"Deb Thomas."

"You asshole!" Taylor slapped the steering wheel. "I told you to leave her out of it! Can't you understand simple English? Asshole!"

After a pause Bonham said softly, "Now I know what's wrong with this picture. You work for us, right?"

"What're you talking about? Don't change the subject."

"You work for us. *We* pay *you*. *You* don't tell *us* what to do."

Taylor's left hand shot out and snapped shut on Bonham's leg just above the knee. He squeezed so hard his hand shook. Bonham choked with the pain and reared back in the seat, stiff, as Taylor kept squeezing.

"Listen, donkey dong. Cut the petty bullshit. When we get to the studio, you call her back. Tell her you made a mistake. Tell her to stay there and I'll pick her up, as planned. Got that? Otherwise, you're gonna have the most expensive recording session you ever saw in your *life*."

EIGHT

The Monday—London (continued)

LATER THAT AFTERNOON when Pat came back from her Hampton Court tour, she walked into their B-and-B and unexpectedly found Tony and a pot of tea waiting. So they sat and sipped while she cheerily told him about her day. Then he grimly told her about his, including the need to go back to the studio for an evening session.

This surprise glitch in their schedule meant revising plans for the rest of the week. They took turns at the telephone making the necessary calls, including one to Stratford to change their theater reservations, and with that out of the way Tony glanced at his watch and said they had time for a quick snack before going back to the studio.

"Good," Pat said. "On my way to the tube station this morning I saw a pub I'd like to try."

They walked along Brompton Road for a block or two till she spotted the pub on the other side of the wide, busy avenue. At the corner they started to cross and almost died.

Stepping off the curb they stood on one of the many signs stenciled in big white letters on London streets: LOOK RIGHT.

Instead, as they always did at home, they looked left. But they were in England, where drivers drive on the wrong side of the road. So, looking left, they didn't see four lanes of high speed London traffic bearing down from the right.

Luckily, London drivers have a sharp eye for tourists and a ready hand on the horn, otherwise Tony and Pat might today be a memorial speed bump on Brompton Road.

At the pub Tony survived another English menace. He ordered steak and kidney pie.

Pat studied him for a long while. "Are you sure?"

"What the heck," he said. "We're here. Let's try it."

"It's fine with me. I was thinking about you." She glanced over the menu. "They have lots of sandwiches. Maybe you'd rather have a sandwich."

"I can have a sandwich any time. But it isn't every day that I have a chance to say, 'Steak and kidney pie.'" He smiled up at the waitress. "And two pints of stout, please."

Fifteen minutes later Pat finished her pie. Tony had taken three bites of his.

Handing Tony the check, the waitress looked down at his plate, frowning at the nearly untouched steak and kidney pie. "They tell me it's an acquired taste," she said. "I wouldn't know, m'self. I've never 'ad the nerve to try it."

Outside on Brompton Road they stood at the edge of the rushing flood of traffic, looking to the right this time. Tony waved down a passing cab, they climbed in, and he gave the driver the studio's name and address on Dean Street.

When the cab was moving again, Pat said, "*In* Dean Street."

Tony glanced at her. "What?"

"*In* Dean Street. That's the way they give addresses in British mysteries. 'We drove to so-and-so *in* Bayswater Road.' Or 'such-and-such address *in* Regent Street.'"

Tony's response, a distracted "Oh" and a nod, told Pat that he was already busy with his recording session, so she settled back beside him and looked out the window as they alternately whizzed and poked along the London's sometimes frantic traffic.

During one of the pokey stretches the cab scarcely moved for several minutes. Tony looked at his watch and sat up on the edge of the seat. "Is there another way that might be faster?" he asked the driver.

The driver glanced in the mirror. "No, sir. The entire city is like this right now, this part of it. Sorry."

Tony sat back again and Pat asked, "Are we late?"

"Not really. Everybody's due at six. But I wanted to get there early to make sure everything's ready to go the minute Taylor walks in."

Pat checked her watch. "It's only five-fifteen."

"I was hoping to get there before the receptionist goes home. She locks the door when she leaves at five. Eric gave me a key but I gave it to Gary Bonham. Figured he could bring the others and let them all in at the same time."

Pat reached over and patted his knee. "Well, hope for the best. Maybe she'll go home and forget to lock up. Maybe the door's stuck and she can't get it locked. Maybe she's working late and the door's still open."

When they pulled up in front of the studio building, it seemed that Pat's first "maybe" was true. Tony pushed on the door and it opened. There was no one in the reception area. "Funny," Tony said. "Eric told me that they always lock up at five. Well, let's go on back."

They walked down the long corridor alongside the main studio and found Eric Richards going into the control room with a couple of twelve-inch tape reels under his arm. Tony introduced Pat and told Eric about the front door being unlocked.

"That's strange," he said. "In fact, I'd say it's impossible, because I locked it myself. Our last session ran a little past five, the receptionist had gone home, and I let the people out. So I know the door was locked then."

"Well, it's unlocked now. If you want, I'll run back up there and lock it."

"Very good of you. And while you're doing that, I'll get your tapes cued up." Eric looked at Pat. "Are you sitting in on Tony's overdub session?"

Tony held up his hands. "Nono. I wouldn't subject her to that." To Pat he said, "I thought you might be interested in strolling through the studio, then you could go out through the doors at the front end and have a seat in the lobby."

"Ah-ha," Pat said. "The old sit-in-the-lobby-and-read-a-magazine-when-I-*could*-be-having-drinks-with-the-Prince-of-Wales routine."

Tony shook his head. "No time for that. We'll only be here an hour."

"In that case, all right."

The door into the studio stood at a right angle to the control booth. Tony pulled it open as he said, "Tell Pat a little about your studio, Eric, and I'll run up front and take care of the front door lock."

Eric smiled. "Delighted," he said, and went into a short, well-oiled bit of patter, after which he let the door whoosh shut behind her and left Pat alone in the very large, nearly dark room.

It gave her a weird feeling. This was the first time she'd been inside a recording studio. Inside the studio itself. She'd sat in lobbies, waiting for Tony. And a couple of times after he'd finished a recording session, she'd gone into a control room and he'd introduced her to engineers and musicians and actors and announcers. But in all the years they'd been married, this was the first time she'd been inside and felt the eerie quiet of a recording studio. And a *London* recording studio, at that.

Eric had told her about some of the famous people who'd recorded here. Olivier. Guinness. Richardson. The Redgraves. "Lots and lots of dramas were done in here. Spooks and ghosts and bodies galore," he'd grinned.

Pat walked slowly across in front of the control room where a wide rectangle of light splashed down through the angled windows onto the waxed vinyl floor and bounced up to make a faint yellow reflection on the ceiling. Tall, thin slivers of light reflected, too, from the stainless steel stems of a little grove of microphone stands crowded into the corner by the window. Otherwise, the studio was dark.

She started back across the room toward the light switches, the sound of her loafers' leather heels on the vinyl floor making an oddly hollow noise, alive but at the same time dead. It was almost eerie.

Then she heard the other footsteps somewhere in the dark studio. She froze, holding her breath. The other steps continued, quiet and quick, almost tiptoe. Staring wide-eyed at the darkness, she whispered, "Hello? Who's there?" From the far end of the studio came a whoosh as the air-lock door moved. A sudden slash of light. A short, hunched shadow squeezed through and the door sighed shut again.

Pat stood in the dark and shook her head. "What's the matter with me?" she muttered to herself. "This is silly. Probably just somebody who works here." She ran to the switches, flipped some lights on, and walked down to the other end of the studio. After going through the two air-lock doorways, she looked around the lobby, saw and heard nothing, and tried the front door to the building. Locked. A deadbolt. "Odd," she muttered again. "Either somebody was in and went out and locked it with a key, or is still in."

She turned and hurried back into the studio. Looking around it from this end, she saw the large wood frame tucked into the angle made by the isolation booth and the main wall. The frame was mounted on casters, so that it could be rolled from place to place, and bolted onto the frame was an ordinary house door. But lined up along the edge of the door, one on top of the other, and screwed onto the door jamb were six different kinds of doorknobs and handles and ten different kinds of locks and bolts, from a modern Yale lock to an old-fashioned skeleton-key lock to a sliding bolt to a metal hasp with a wood peg.

Set into the floor in front of the door were six wood boxes about two feet square, their tops level with the floor. The first was filled with sand. The next with gravel. The next, slate. The next square had a piece of heavy-looking metal inset. The next had flooring tile, and the last had wood parquet.

Walking slowly along, Pat looked down at the boxes. In one, the surface of the sand seemed scuffed up and a thin layer of sand had spilled onto the floor around it. Her shoes grated on the sandy floor and she stopped, smiling. "Sound effects!" she said. "For making different kinds of footsteps." She looked at the door. "And a sound effects door! Different locks and openers for different kinds of doors. Isn't that clever!"

Smiling to herself, she reached across the row of boxes to the door and turned the knob on the deadbolt. The door flew open in her face and she screamed as a man jumped out. He fell and his head hit Pat's right shoulder and knocked her backwards as he thudded to the floor at her feet. His face crunched in the sand box. Pat caught her breath and screamed again. "Tony!"

She twisted her head toward the control room and realized that it was still only Eric and that he couldn't hear a thing through the glass. She ran to the window, pounding it with her fists till the vibration or the motion caught his attention. Eric turned and jumped when he saw her terrified face.

He ran out of the control room and into the studio. She grabbed his hand and pulled him to the sound effects corner, where he looked down at the body and said, "How the hell did *he* get in here?"

At that moment the front door of the studio opened and Tony walked in.

NINE

The Monday (continued)

WHEN TONY PUSHED the heavy studio door open he expected to see his wife exploring the big room with that eager, inquisitive expression she always wore when she discovered something new. So when he bounced in and saw Pat's pale frightened face, the surprise stopped him in his tracks. Behind him, the door whooshed shut. The sound could have been his own breath being taken away.

Pat turned toward him, her eyes full of fear and confusion. She raised a hand and reached for him. He ran to her across the room and for the first time noticed Eric on one knee behind her and then the twisted pile of a man lying face down in the scattered sand. It was Gary Bonham.

Tony took Pat in his arms and held her, stroking her head with one hand and her back with the other. "What is it? What happened?"

"I don't know, I don't know," she mumbled into his chest. Blindly she waved toward the sound effects door along the wall. "I just opened that door and he fell out."

"Is he all right?" Tony asked Eric over Pat's head but she said, "I don't know, I don't know, I didn't stop to check." She stepped back and took a deep breath. "But we'd better do it." She turned and dropped to one knee beside the body.

Tony knelt with her. "I'll do it."

Pat shook her head once. "It's okay. I'm all right."

As she reached out to touch the artery in Bonham's neck, a voice yelled, "What the hell's going on!"

Pat jerked back. "Ohmygod!"

Eric turned to look at the studio's front door. "Your client," he said, surprise in his voice. "Norris."

Tony ignored Chet Norris. On one knee by the body he touched the base of Bonham's throat, then the side of his neck. "Can't feel a thing," he said, almost to himself. "No pulse, nothing."

"I said, what's going on!" Norris let the door slide shut and started across the patio.

"Shouldn't we call the police?" Pat looked at Tony, at Eric and back to Tony.

"When did Bonham come back?" Tony asked Eric.

Eric shrugged. "I have no idea. Didn't know he was here till I heard your wife give a shout."

"Tony, let's call the—"

Norris stopped beside Pat and said, "What do you have to do to get an answer around here?"

"I wonder the same thing."

"Good God!" Norris said suddenly. "What's the matter with Bonham? What happened?"

"We don't know," Tony said. "How long have you been here, Chet?"

"Tony!" Pat almost stamped her foot. "Just call the police and let them handle it."

"Right. You're right." Tony nodded and said to Eric, "Will you call? Tell them they'll need an ambulance, too." Eric hurried toward the control room and Tony turned to Norris again. "When did you say you got here?"

"I didn't. When did you suddenly become a cop?"

"I didn't. But when they get here they'll want to know when *we* got here and where we've been, so we ought to have the information ready for—"

Suddenly the studio door swung open again. Paul Taylor burst through and held it open for Deb Thomas. "Let the session begin!" Taylor boomed, and then they both stared across the studio at the body on the floor.

"Good heavens!" Deb cried. "What happened?"

DETECTIVE INSPECTOR Vincent Pomeroy asked the same question when he arrived a few minutes later with a sergeant and two uniformed officers in response to Eric's call.

But before he asked the question, Inspector Pomeroy walked slowly around the body, murmuring comments to the sergeant.

The sergeant sat on his heels beside the body. After pulling on a pair of thin clear plastic gloves, he carefully searched Bonham's pockets, every now and then interrupting the quiet mumble of their conversation to hand something up to the inspector—a slip of paper, a wallet with a passport tucked inside, a pocket calendar.

Pomeroy held each item lightly, by the edges, scanning it quickly before passing it on to an officer trailing behind him, who dropped it into a clear plastic bag.

But Pomeroy kept the calendar. Fanning through the pages, he stopped, studied an entry, then closed the little book around a ballpoint pen to mark his place. He slipped the calendar into his pocket and crossed the studio to the group of silent watchers.

"Now then," he said. "What happened?"

Inspector Pomeroy directed the question to Eric. In fact, as soon as he realized that all the others were Americans, Inspector Pomeroy spoke at first only to Eric, as though afraid of bumping into a language barrier if he tried to talk with anyone from the United States.

Eric told him about being in the control room, about hearing Pat's frantic thump-thump-thump on the window, about rushing into the studio where she showed him the body, "...and then Tony—Mr. Pratt—came into the studio from the reception area."

"'Studio,'" the inspector said, looking around the big, bare room. "I'm afraid I'm not clear on exactly what sort of business you carry on here?"

By this time the medical examiner, laboratory technicians and a photographer had come in and begun bustling around the body like birds at a feeder.

The photographer seemed especially distracting, to Deb Thomas and Pat Pratt particularly. Each time his camera popped and flashed, they jerked their heads away and squeezed their eyes shut or covered them with their hands.

And when the medical examiner stooped over Bonham's body, when he began moving arms and legs and head, when he tugged Bonham's tie loose and started to unbutton his shirt, Deb turned aside and into Paul Taylor's arms for comfort.

Chet Norris looked at her and all but sneered. "Ah, what have we here? A new-found pro-tec-tor?"

Taylor ignored him. Instead, he said to Inspector Pomeroy, "Look, Lieutenant—"

"Inspector—"

"Inspector. Sorry. Can we get out of here?"

"I beg your pardon?"

"Do we have to stay here in the studio? This may be routine for you, but not for us. Can't we go someplace, out to the lobby or to one of the offices or—"

"Oh, of course, of course, by all means, of course. Forgive me." And he let Eric shepherd everyone out of the studio and along the corridor to the clients' lounge and its "more congenial atmosphere," as he called it.

The only objection came from Chet Norris. "Wait a minute! Let's just stay put and get this over with. I've got to take off."

"I'm afraid that may not be possible, sir."

"What the hell do you mean, 'that may not be possible'! What kind of a game is this? A guy drops dead of a heart attack or something and it's a big deal? I've got business to take care of, appointments to keep! I've got to catch a train for—"

"Well, sir, let's just see how things sort themselves out, shall we?" and the inspector held out a hand, ushering Norris on into the lounge.

Pomeroy watched while they settled themselves around the little room—Deb Thomas and Paul

Taylor on the wicker love seat, Chet Norris and Pat each in one of the wicker chairs, Tony and Eric standing—and then he looked directly at Eric. "I haven't yet had a response to my earlier comment. I said that I'm not clear on just what sort of business is carried on here. Perhaps you would enlighten me."

"These are recording studios," Eric answered. "We record motion picture and television sound tracks, radio commercials, that sort of thing."

Finally Inspector Pomeroy scanned the others and said, "And the rest of you—Americans all, as I take it—why are you here? Is this some kind of tour?"

A little surge of laughter rose and fell, and Tony said, "No, it's not a tour, Lieutenant—"

"Inspector—"

"Excuse me—Inspector. No, we're here to work."

Deborah Thomas and Paul Taylor in different ways simultaneously gave the same answer, but Pat said, "I'm a mere bystander, here with my husband"—she nodded toward Tony—"who is not going to get involved."

Somewhat surprised by her remark, Pomeroy looked closely at Pat, and in the silence Chet Norris said, "The only reason I'm here is that I got a message at the hotel from Miss Thomas. There was also a message from Mr. Pratt. However, Miss Thomas is the only one who could get me back to this place.''

" 'Back to this place'?'' Pomeroy tilted an eyebrow. '' 'Back'? You were here earlier?''

Deb said, ''Yes, we were all here this morning.'' She frowned at Norris and added quickly, ''I didn't call. I didn't leave a message for you.''

''Neither did I,'' Tony said. ''What time was it? Did you actually *see* a message?''

''Tony!'' Pat's voice was sharp but she smiled as she spoke, the kind of smile a bridge player smiles just after she kicks her partner under the table. ''Please. Do not. Get. Involved.''

Again Inspector Pomeroy gazed at Pat, but this time his expression was one of confused innocence.

''Inspector,'' Tony said, ''maybe I can explain some of this. We were here this morning for a recording session. We weren't able to finish the job, so we came back to wrap it up tonight.''

''Isn't this an odd time of day to be working?''

The policeman seemed surprised as a new wave of smiles swept around the room before Eric said, ''No, Inspector, *no* time of day is an odd time of day in this business. We've been known to work twenty-four hours a day.''

''So. The building is open twenty-four hours a day?''

"Oh, no," Eric said. "The outside doors, the doors to the building, are locked every day at five."

One by one, Pomeroy looked at each person in the room. But he spoke to Eric. "So. When people come to work here after five o'clock, you give them all keys?"

Eric shook his head. "Not at all. There's a bell-push by the door frame in front. In the usual case, people coming for jobs after five give a buzz and get let in."

" 'In the usual case,' you say. Is this an '*un*usual case'?"

"In a way, yes. For one of our ordinary sessions we have people coming from all over London, coming from different directions and due at different times. But these people are visitors. They come in together, all at the same time and all from the same hotel, most of them. So I gave a key to Tony—Mr. Pratt—so he could let 'em all in."

The inspector turned to Tony. "Is that right?"

"That's right."

"And you have it?"

A quick, embarrassed smile came over Tony's face. "Well, no. As I told Eric, I planned to get here early and so I gave the key to Gary Bonham, figuring that he would bring the others."

"So." Pomeroy stared at Tony and the silence seemed to last for a long, long time. "You gave the key to the victim?"

"Yes."

"That's very curious."

"Why?"

There was another, shorter silence before Pomeroy said, "He had no keys."

"What?"

"He had no keys. I'll mention another curious thing, Mr. Pratt." The inspector slipped his right hand into the side pocket of his tweed jacket. "You say that you left no message for Mr. Norris?"

"That's right, Lieutenant."

"Inspector."

"Inspector. Sorry."

"Perhaps it was Mr. Bonham for whom you left a message."

Tony shook his head. "No. And no message for Gary Bonham, either."

"Well, perhaps you can explain this entry in Mr. Bonham's calendar." He pulled out the little leather-covered book and let several pages flip past his thumb till he found the entry. "Under today's date it reads, as near as I can make out, 'To studio early PM per T. Pratt call.'" Inspector Pomeroy held the calendar out for Tony to see. "Now. I find that curious also, Mr. Pratt. What do you suppose it means?"

TEN

The Monday (continued)

BEFORE TONY COULD answer Pomeroy, a uniformed officer stepped into the open doorway and touched a finger to the brim of his bobby helmet in a sort of waving salute. "I beg your pardon, Inspector, but the medical people would like a word."

"Ah," said Pomeroy, "thank you." He politely excused himself—from the room in general and no one in particular—and hurried away, his pudgy face brightly expectant.

But it looked very different a few minutes later. He came back into the room slowly, head studiously down, as if watching for potholes in the vinyl floor. He wore an odd, distracted expression when he raised his head and looked directly at Tony for his answer to the question. "You were saying, sir, about your call to Mr. Bonham?"

"I was about to say that I didn't call him and I didn't leave a message for him to meet me. I didn't call him or talk to him after the session broke up this morning."

"I can vouch for that," Pat put in abruptly.

The inspector tilted his head back slightly and seemed to peer around his nose at Pat. "You were together all the time?"

She looked at Tony and he looked at her and they both turned to the inspector and at the same time she said, "Yes" and he said, "No."

They looked at each other again and she said, "What did you say?"

"I said, 'No.'"

"I said, 'Yes.'"

"I know," Tony said. "Why?"

"Trying to help."

"Do I need help?"

"He seems to think you need an alibi."

"Why do I need an alibi? And what are you smiling about? This isn't funny. Gary Bonham's on the floor in there, dead."

"I know it isn't funny. But the idea that you shot him is so silly that I—"

"Mrs.—uh—Pratt, is it? Yes. Might we begin again, and this time I'd prefer to let Mr. Pratt provide his own answers, if you don't mind. In fact, Mr. Pratt, perhaps we could just step down the corridor, you and I, to one of the offices we passed earlier."

Inspector Pomeroy's gaze took in the others in the room as he said, "And if you will just try to make yourselves comfortable, please, we'll do our

best to make your time here as brief as possible.''
He held out a hand as if showing Tony to the door,
but he stopped and said, "And for your information, Mrs. Pratt, Mr. Bonham wasn't shot.''

Pomeroy ushered Tony into the hall and at the
same time signaled to the uniformed officer, who
planted himself in the doorway, the top of his tall
helmet disappearing above the frame.

In the office to the right of the clients' lounge,
Pomeroy leaned his rump against the desk, but before he could speak, Tony blurted, "He wasn't
shot?''

"No, sir.''

"What killed him, then?''

"That's all I'm free to tell you for the moment,
sir, I'm afraid. Now let's turn things front-end-to,
if you don't mind, so that I'm the one asking the
questions.'' A touch of a smile tugged the corner of
Pomeroy's mouth. "A sequence that Mrs. Pratt
would approve, I'm sure.''

Tony answered that with a half-smile of his own
and the inspector continued. "Now then. First of
all, you were a friend of the victim?''

"A 'business friend' might be more accurate. I
was a partner in an advertising agency in San
Francisco; we sold it about four years ago; Gary
was one of the four people who bought it.''

"And you hadn't seen him since that time?''

"Oh, yes. Since then, I've done several free-lance jobs for Gary and the agency, because I know some of the accounts very well. But I didn't have any contact with him except when I had a job to do for the agency."

"I see. And you were saying that you didn't call or leave a message for Mr. Bonham?"

"That's right, Lieuten—Inspector. I didn't see or talk with Gary after our session broke up this morning."

"'Session'?"

"Recording session."

"Ah, yes. Every business seems to have its own jargon, doesn't it? So. You said earlier that you didn't finish your work this morning?"

"Yes, that's why we'd planned to finish tonight."

"Which is obviously out of the question, of course."

"So we'll try to do it tomorrow, I guess."

"I'm afraid that won't do either, sir. We're shutting down activities here for a while. I hope it isn't too much of an inconvenience."

"Shut down! For how long? We came all this way and—"

"Yes, I see that. And, as I said, I'm sorry for the inconvenience, but that's the way it is. So. Getting back to this morning. You also said earlier, and repeated here, that your 'session' broke up. Should I infer that something happened, something went wrong?''

"Did something go wrong!" Tony's laugh somehow sounded both humorless and sarcastic.

"Just tell me what happened, please.''

Once started, Tony poured out the story as if he'd been waiting a week to tell it. It was "the lousiest little recording session I've even been involved in," he said. He described Chet Norris's constant interference, Gary Bonham's unwillingness to step in and control his client, and Paul Taylor's obedient following of directions. Up to a point.

And then, with a happy smile, Tony told how Taylor ripped into Norris and walked out. He wound up with Norris threatening Bonham and his agency and, finally, firing Tony.

"One more thing," he added. "While all this crap was going on, I got the idea that there was something underneath, something more than just screwing up a recording session.''

Inspector Pomeroy leaned against the desk and looked down at the scuffed round tips of his black shoes. "Such a jolly little family group," he said. "Sounds as though there's a bit of motive there for everyone, doesn't it?" He peered at Tony. "Including you."

"Me!" Tony's jaw dropped.

"Yes, sir. You expect Mr. Bonham to control his client, thereby protecting you. He fails to do so. You resent it. Confront him. He, in turn, resents your accusations."

"And I shoot him?"

Pomeroy raised a finger. "He wasn't shot, Mr. Pratt. Remember, sir?"

Before Tony could answer, a roar of angry voices came from the next room. He heard Pat yell. Another woman screamed and a man shouted, "Here, now, none of that!" Then there was a thump and the room shivered, and two pictures dropped off the office wall and shattered. Tony and the inspector ran out the door, down the hall, and into the lounge.

Pat stood alone in the center of the room. Deb Thomas and Paul Taylor stood behind the love seat, their arms around each other. Eric and the uniformed officer were bending over Chet Norris, who lay crumpled against the wall, blood dribbling from his nose and mouth.

Tony rushed over to Pat. Inspector Pomeroy kept going to check on Norris, and Tony heard the uniformed officer say, "Strong as a bull, the little man must be, Inspector." His tall helmet wagged back and forth in wonder.

"This fellow all right, do you think?"

"I think so, sir. Although I never saw a man hit so bloody hard in my life. In the air, he was, when he hit the wall."

"Go see if the medical types are still out front, and bring someone back here. See if they can put him back together."

"Yes, sir."

The medical types were there and they did "put Norris back together."

They stopped the bleeding and salved his bruises—"He must have given himself a nosebleed when he hit the wall," Taylor said. "All I did was punch him in the gut. And the shoulder. I never hit anybody in the face. Too hard on your hands."—and they even took him back to the hotel after he sullenly answered Pomeroy's questions.

The inspector then resumed his interviews with Pat, Deb, Taylor and Eric, too. They each had a session with him in the office next door, each meeting getting noticeably shorter than the one before, and when he'd finished with Eric, he gathered them all in the lounge again. There the inspector confirmed closing the studio "until further notice."

Eric looked up at the inspector from his seat in one of the wicker chairs. "What exactly does that mean, Inspector? One day? Two days? Week?"

"I can't honestly answer that. I would estimate two days, possibly only one. We'll just have to see how it goes, day by day, as they say." Pomeroy started to turn away, stopped and looked down at Eric to say in a much softer tone, "I hope your business doesn't suffer too much. Can't be avoided, you know."

"Can't be helped, I suppose." Eric seemed at a loss for words. "Well!" he finally said. He slapped his hands on his knees and pushed himself to his feet. "I have a lot of telephoning to do, recording sessions to re-book. Am I free to go? Is that all?"

Pomeroy nodded. "Yes, but please tell me if you plan to leave the city."

Walking out of the room, Eric looked back and said sarcastically, "Not bloody likely."

The inspector watched Eric leave but spoke to the others, raising his voice a little. "That applies to the rest of you ladies and gentlemen. That's all for now. Feel free to leave, but please let us know any travel plans you may have."

Deb Thomas looked at Taylor and then said to the inspector, "If it's possible, I'd like to see if I can keep the business appointment Mr. Norris made for tomorrow in Leeds. It could be very important for our company."

"I think that would be acceptable. Just leave your itinerary and where you can be reached, should that become necessary."

Pomeroy studied the tips of his shoes again. He seemed to have dismissed them, his last words trailing off, as if he'd spoken to a student who'd lagged behind to ask an unnecessary question.

"Mrs. Pratt and I have reservations for a play in Stratford tomorrow evening."

The sound of Tony's voice seemed to raise Pomeroy's head, slowly. "Ah," he said. "Mr. Pratt." The inspector's head turned toward Tony but his eyes examined Pat's pale face for a second or two. "Stratford? I think that would be acceptable. As a matter of fact, getting away for a bit might be a very sound idea. But I would like to see you in my office on Wednesday. So, again, leave your itinerary with the officer outside. And please, don't try to leave the country."

ELEVEN

The Monday (continued)

THERE HAD BEEN her sudden scream of shock when Bonham's body fell at Pat's feet. There was the quick uproar when Paul Taylor punched Chet Norris into the wall. Except for those few spikey seconds, the past three hours had been spent in the recording studio's abnormal, almost suffocating quiet. The police, even, with their laboratory technicians and medical people, had done their grim business in a kind of hush.

So when Tony and Pat stepped out into the busy London night, they flinched at the noise. Their noses twitched at the smoke and fumes from cars and trucks and the still-hot street.

They turned left, without a word or any particular reason, walking slowly down the crowded sidewalk. Behind them, holding hands, Deb Thomas and Paul Taylor followed quietly, Taylor smiling to himself. He squeezed Deb's hand and pointed to a four-story brick building across the street. Its ground floor held an Italian restaurant named *Quo Vadis*. On the first of a row of flats next to *Quo Vadis*, a small, round blue plaque read:

KARL MARX
1818-1883
LIVED HERE
1851-1856

They walked on toward Oxford Circus past a chemist's shop, a Korean restaurant, the Detroit Clothing Company, and a pub advertising SPLENDID HOME-COOKED FOOD, GOULASH AT ALL HOURS, past a building housing an ENGLISH AND COMPUTER SCHOOL, and a black-windowed storefront with a yellow and red sign on the door: LIVE THE 80'S WITH A SENSUAL EXOTIC EXPERIENCE.

"Hey!" Taylor yelled. Tony and Pat looked back. He waved and started for the door. "Don't wait up!"

Deb grabbed his arm and tugged him up to the corner where Tony and Pat stood beside a parked cab. Taylor shrugged. "It was just a thought." Then he pointed to the cab and said, in fake surprise, "Well, look what we found." He reached into his pocket and pulled out his keys. "Taylor's Londinium Taxi."

"I'll be damned," Tony said.

Taylor looked at him. "You didn't know my car was here?"

"How would I know that?"

Taylor frowned at Deb. "Right, Deborah, how would he know that?" He turned to Pat. "Well, your prize for finding it is a ride home. And I think you can use it. You look like a lady who's had a spooky afternoon. Crawl in."

Pat let her shoulders sag. "You're right. I accept."

He held the rear door open for her, and as she got in Tony asked, "D'you know where we're going?"

"I'll know as soon as you tell me, Your Producership."

"You know Harrod's?"

"One of my wives almost bought it."

"When you get to Harrod's, turn right."

"Got it. Hop in."

With everyone inside, Deb Thomas leaned over from her seat in the swivel chair and said quietly in Taylor's ear, "After what happened today, I think you might be a little more serious."

Before she could sit back, Taylor turned and kissed her quickly on the mouth, then he swung around a little more, so that he could see everyone in the car. "All right, everybody. Listen up," he said in his most announcerish voice. "This is your captain speaking."

"Paul!"

His voice relaxed. "I didn't know Bonham as well as most of you knew him or I might feel more affected. Or if he'd been a different kind of guy, maybe I'd feel more affected. The way I feel is, I'm sorry he died but there's not one damned thing I can do about it now. If you're sad, I'll respect that. As for me, I do not and cannot feel mournful and I don't intend to fake it." He turned in his seat and started his car.

Deb stared at him for a second or two, then she leaned over again and kissed him quickly on the ear.

"To Harrod's," he said.

In the back seat, Tony and Pat held hands and said nothing.

It was a quiet ride. That is, as quiet as a ride can be in London on a warm, late-summer evening.

Then they turned onto wide, busy Brompton Road. Three blocks from Harrod's Taylor was caught by a traffic signal. In the front rank of four lanes of traffic, Taylor sat and watched a flood of people wash past in the pedestrian lane, a thick and endless river.

The light changed but the river flowed on. A few drivers honked. The stream of pedestrians thinned, otherwise the current stayed steady. Taylor tried to move forward. Scowling, people kept coming.

"All right," he said. He shoved a tape into the tape deck and grabbed the microphone clipped to the dash beside it.

Suddenly, the pedestrian river froze. The frightening rumble and roar of a thousand stampeding cattle thundered down Brompton Road, a bawling wild-eyed herd bearing down on Harrod's.

Over the thundering hooves a bugle blared the cavalry "Charge!"

The pedestrian river thawed, cracked in the center and began to pull back toward its banks.

Another bugle call. "Charge!"

People backed away faster. They stumbled over each other. Desperate eyes looked in every direction, even up in the air, trying to find the churning, mindless herd of Texas longhorns and the equally mindless troop of cavalry charging down Brompton Road. Somewhere.

In his taxi, Taylor slid the sunroof back and stood on his seat. A few of the scattering people stopped and stared.

They saw a grizzled head and broad shoulders suddenly appear through the top of an ordinary London taxi. They saw Taylor wave his hand over his head and point forward. But what they heard above the thundering charge was John Wayne, booming through the speaker. "A-Troop! Right by twos! Yo-o! Stand aside, pilgrim!"

With Brompton Road cleared of pedestrians, Taylor's taxi drove away, riding point.

TAYLOR TURNED OFF Brompton Road at Harrod's. In front of their B-and-B, Tony and Pat stood on the curb by the driver's side to say goodnight.

"Oh, by the way," Taylor said, "here." He held his hand out to Tony with a key standing up between his thumb and first finger. "I didn't want to embarrass you in front of the cop."

Tony took it and stared at the shiny piece of metal in the center of his palm. Curious, Pat crowded close as Taylor drove away. "What is it?"

"The key to the studio. The one I gave to Gary Bonham."

TWELVE

Tuesday—Oxford and Stratford

VERY EARLY ON A gray Tuesday morning, Tony and Pat crossed the platform at Paddington Station and boarded a train for Oxford.

"We've scheduled a couple of very full days for ourselves, you know," Tony said. He picked a couple of empty seats, dropped his garment bag on one, and slid past it to sit by the window.

Pat sat facing him across a small table between their knee-to-knee seats. "It'll be fun," she said. "Lots of new things to see."

They planned to rent a car in Oxford and drive through the Cotswolds to Stratford-on-Avon. "Stratford-*Upon*-Avon," as Pat corrected herself. They'd see *Othello* that evening, then stay overnight at another bed-and-breakfast that she'd heard about, in a village called Chadlington. Early Wednesday morning they'd drive back to Oxford, return the car, and take the train back to London, arriving in time for Tony's interview with Inspector Pomeroy at Scotland Yard.

"Busy," Tony said. "Busy, busy, busy."

"Well, if you'd rent a car here in London, we could skip this train ride. The only reason we're going to Oxford is because you won't rent a car in London."

"And the only reason I won't rent a car in London is because I'm trying to save your life." He wagged his head. "Me? Drive in this traffic? With all those crazy traffic circles?"

"'Roundabouts,' they're called." She smiled out the window. "Look. We're moving."

"Didn't even feel it." He nodded, watching the platform and the smoky steel girders glide past. "Smooth."

Pat gazed at the tail end of the train curling out of the station. "We have roundabouts in Oregon."

Tony frowned.

"Yes," she said. "In Portland. And you drive through them without even thinking about it."

"I've never seen one. Where?"

"On the east side. Ladd's Addition. And on the way to Providence Hospital."

"Oh, those. Those little two-lane circles're nothing. *These* things are like whirlpools. Five lanes wide, going around in circles ninety miles an hour. Get caught in there and you'll sink without a trace." He shook his head. "Crazy."

"You could do it."

"Maybe. But first I'll rent a car in Oxford. Practice on the rest of the country." He stared out the window for a few seconds.

The train rolled behind a row of tall, dirty brick buildings. Narrow wooden porches marked each floor. Gray, soggy laundry sagged on limp ropes that drooped from the corner posts. Rickety wooden stairs dripped down their backsides, as if the porches were leaking. Crowded together, the buildings seemed to be huddling in self-protection against the new industrial plants creeping in from all sides.

"Another thing," he said to the window. "I told them I want a car with automatic transmission. I'll be driving on the wrong side of the road, sitting on the wrong side of the car, and I sure as hell don't want to be trying to shift gears with the wrong hand."

"You'll be fine."

"Right," Tony said. "I'll be fine. Driving on the wrong side of the road for the first time." He gave her a serious look. "I notice you signed up for extra insurance."

She looked right back, not sure whether to laugh or scream. "I did not!"

He smiled. "Then do it when we get the car."

"Oh, stop."

He turned to the window again and without a pause said, "I'd still like to know when Bonham showed up at the studio. And how Paul Taylor got that key."

"Stop that, too. It's Inspector Pomeroy's job, let him do it."

Past Tony's shoulder she saw one of the train porters pushing a small serving cart down the aisle. "Ah-ha," she said, "refreshments."

Fifteen minutes out of London they snacked on tea and scones as the train whizzed past a wide, newly-furrowed field with cattle feeding beside a rough stone shed. Pale sunlight seeped through a thin spot in the overcast. It seemed unlikely to last. Tentative and disinterested, it made weak and watery shadows in the field's deep furrows.

They crossed a river with a village growing along its banks. In the odd sunlight, the brick houses and red tile roofs lost their color and seemed flat. In the river, beautiful wood ducks dabbled in the water around a small, weedy island.

One seat ahead of Tony and Pat and on the other side of the aisle, a woman filed her nails while her husband read *The International Herald-Tribune*. Behind the paper he gave a sour laugh but she didn't look up. "The Cubs have lost eight games in a row," he said.

She stretched out one hand, frowning at the nails. "How long to Oxford?"

"The Forty-Niners beat the Bears, 36-zip. Got another dog on our hands."

She flexed her fingers and buffed her nails on her breast. "How long to Oxford?"

The man stayed behind the newspaper. "Twelve days. What am I, a tour director?" He folded the paper in half and studied the box scores.

She shifted the nail file to her other hand. Glaring at the stone wall of his newspaper, she made an ugly face and mouthed his last words, "What am I, a tour director?"

Watching out the window, Tony and Pat enjoyed the scenery. "Looks like home," she smiled. Except for the town names—Reading, Pangbourne, Abingdon—and fences of stone instead of wood and wire, the English countryside could have been Oregon's Willamette Valley.

Farms with broad, undulating fields, brown and stubbled, were dotted with giant rolls of hay that had been cut and wound into tight round bales. They looked like the farms around Salem in late summer.

Nearing Oxford, wide patches of black, burnt-over fields bordered by poplars could have been the grass-seed fields in southern Oregon, where the growers burn their fields after harvest.

"The trees are different, though," Pat said, standing beside Tony as the train came to a stop at the Oxford station.

"Right," he said, "I don't see any firs."

AT THE CAR rental agency—"car hire centre," Pat noted—the pretty young woman behind the counter smiled apologetically at Tony. "I'm sorry. There were no left-hand drives available," she said. "But we did find an automatic for you."

"Good," Tony grinned. "That's a relief."

"It may just be the last one in Britain. May I show you the drill?"

He looked up from signing the form. "What?"

"She wants to show us how it works," Pat translated.

Dodging four or five other people lined up at the counter, they followed the clerk out the side door of the station to a row of red Ford Fiestas. They stopped at the first one and Tony tossed his garment bag on the back seat, aware of two people loading luggage into the next car in line.

The clerk opened the right-hand door and held it open for Tony. He sat behind the steering wheel. Pat walked around to the left-hand side and sat in the front passenger seat, leaning back in the seat, testing.

In the open door on the driver's side, the clerk bent down cheek to cheek with Tony, her left hand resting on his shoulder. Pat sat up and watched.

The clerk brushed her right hand along the steering column and across the dashboard. "Ignition, there. Lights. Oil, petrol, and so on."

She dropped her hand to his knee and pointed to the floor. "The pedals are in the same configuration that you're accustomed to. The turn indicators, windscreen wash, and bright beams are also the same. The only difference is, the shifting lever is on the floor on your left instead of your right. But that shouldn't be a bother, since it's automatic."

She slid her hand down his leg to the front of the seat. "Seat adjustment under the seat front." She tugged and his seat jerked backwards. Patting his thigh she said, "Sorry about that."

Her hand searched along the door frame as she went on, "Safety strap above the door"—pulling it down she stretched it across Tony's belly—"attaching just below your left hip. There," she said, giving him a gentle tap.

She backed out of the car and straightened, tugging her skirt down. "And that's the lot. All set, then?"

"I think so," Tony said, looking her up and down. "Thank you very much."

"Thank you," she smiled. "And good luck."

He watched her walk away.

Pat said, "Friendly."

"Yes," he said. "Very nice." He slid the key into the ignition. "Perhaps I can drop you somewhere and catch you up later?" he said. "The greengrocer? The chemist? The flicks?"

"Drive."

He started the car but then hopped out to take off his jacket and drop it on the back seat on top of his bag. As he closed the rear door, he noticed the next-door Ford. It was rented by the same couple who'd been on the train.

Still working on her fingernails, the woman was in the passenger seat on the left-hand side. The man stowed the last piece of luggage and slammed the trunk lid down. He went around to the left front door, yanked it open, and sat on his wife's lap.

They both yelped and he jumped out. "Shees!" he said, looking across the roof of his car at Tony. "What the hell're we doin' here, buddy?"

ONCE HE STARTED driving, the conversation between Tony and Pat was limited. "Turn here." "Take the next right." "Well, if we missed it, we'll just have to go back and find it." And a few of Tony's Anglo-Saxon specialties.

It was a learning experience for both.

For one thing, Pat learned the flip side of Winston Churchill's famous "V for Victory" symbol. Displayed with the palm turned outward, it's the familiar V. But displayed with the palm turned inward, it's the English driver's version of America's famous Finger.

Pat returned the gesture three or four times with a big, friendly smile before she realized the difference.

But with an Ordnance Survey map open on her lap, she navigated them through several roundabouts and across the ring road around Oxford.

Past the ring road and on the A-34 heading north toward Stratford, Tony seemed to relax a little. He wiggled around in the seat, stretched, and rested his hand on her leg. "I like a small car," he said. "Keeps you close."

She rubbed his hand and smiled. "Feel more comfortable now?"

"About driving on the wrong side?" He nodded. "It'll take some getting used to but it's really not that bad."

"Good."

After another silence he said, "You know what I've been thinking?"

"Yes."

"I wonder when Gary Bonham showed up at the studio."

"Yes."

"You, too?"

"No. I mean, I know it's on your mind. And I wish you'd try to forget about it. Leave it for the police."

"I can't. You know that Pomeroy thinks I might have a motive?—thinks I might have had something to do with it?"

"You're not serious."

"You heard him! 'Well, Mr. Pratt, you say you didn't leave a message for Mr. Bonham? Then perhaps you can explain this note on his calendar, Mr. Pratt?'"

"He's probably just—what do they call it? 'Fishing.' He's probably just fishing, trying to find *something*."

"Maybe. But I'd better find some answers before he figures I'm his fish."

"Please." Pat shook her head and went back to her map.

"That key is another thing. How the hell did Paul Taylor get that key? Did he take it from Bonham? Did Taylor go to the studio with Bonham?"

"I don't know. Oh, look!" she said suddenly, pointing. "That road sign said 'Kidlington.'"

"What's that?"

"Morse's headquarters."

"Morse?"

"Chief Inspector Morse. Thames Valley Police. He's the main character in Colin Dexter's books. You've read some—drives a Lancia? In the books it's a Lancia but on television it's a Jaguar."

Tony shrugged. "If you see him, tell him to find out who killed Bonham. And why. And why he left a message with my name on it."

"Who says it's a 'he'? Maybe it's a 'she.' Oh, stop!"

"What?"

"Now you've got *me* doing it! Leave it for the police. Give. It. Up. Please!"

For a long, long time the car was quiet except for the engine. They didn't even comment when they drove right past Blenheim Palace and didn't stop to see Churchill's home.

THIRTEEN

Tuesday Evening—Stratford

THEY ARRIVED IN Stratford safely, slightly harried but whole, a little later than planned.

They'd stopped briefly in the village of Chadlington, at the bed-and-breakfast where they had reservations that night. Because they wouldn't get out of the theater and back to the B-and-B until very late, they decided to pick up the key on the way to Stratford.

Chadlington was away from the main roads in the Cotswolds, but Tony and Pat had no trouble finding the B-and-B. Except for the church and a few barns, it was the only two-story building in the village.

Mrs. Peterson, the owner, showed them the room.

"Lovely," Pat said.

Tony gave the room a quick glance. "Private bath?"

Mrs. Peterson smiled a smile that was very close to a laugh. "Oh, yes," she said, opening a door beside the closet. "The bath." Her broad English "A" made it sound like "bawth."

"You Americans and your *bawth*," she said. "You're always *bawthing*. It's a wonder there's anything of you left!"

At Stratford, Tony and Pat looked along the River Avon. Cool and dark, green under the arching trees, the river surface folded slowly on itself, curling into long rippling strands. Downstream, a stone church tower stood, patient and old.

"There's a river that was never meant to be a neighbor to a parking lot."

"*No* river was meant to be a neighbor to a parking lot," his wife said.

"True."

But there was the CAR PARK sign. He maneuvered the little Ford through the crowd to a vacant slot.

Getting out of the car, they both stood arching their backs and stretching when a sudden blast of big-band music ripped through the air. Jolted, like everyone else, by the unexpected sound of Johnny Carson's brassy theme song tearing the air over Shakespeare's birthplace, they looked around, trying to find out where it was coming from. Then a voice like Ed McMahon's boomed out, "And now, ladies and gentlemen, heeee-re's Tony!"

Preceded by whistles and applause, a London taxi drove slowly down the center aisle of the busy parking lot.

The Americans in the crowd grinned at each other and shrugged off another peculiar example of English eccentricity.

The English in the crowd regarded each other with stone-faced acceptance of another American's gaudy flamboyance.

Paul Taylor and Deb Thomas ignored both attitudes and waved at Tony and Pat.

Tony waved back and said, "Where the hell did they come from?"

Pat waved and said, "Same place we did. And don't start right in asking a lot of questions."

"Don't worry," he said. "You know me better than that."

"Of course."

They waited for Taylor to park his cab. When he and Deb walked up, Pat said, "What a surprise."

Taylor and Deb said, "Hi."

Tony said, "How the hell did you get that key?"

HE LEARNED SEVERAL other things before he got an answer, and when the answer came, it had some other stories wrapped around it.

Chet Norris had tried to shake down Taylor's agent and threatened to ruin Taylor's reputation with other advertisers.

Deb Thomas suspected that Norris was taking kickbacks from Thomas Baking Company's suppliers; she was debating whether to tell her father about her suspicions or confront Norris directly.

Hearing those stories, Tony wondered whether Norris had been bleeding Gary Bonham's advertising agency; if that might explain why Bonham had been so worried lately, why he'd been drinking so much. But when he asked the question, nobody answered.

Instead, Taylor said that he'd told Deb not to let Norris know she suspected he was taking kickbacks.

Deb said they'd been arguing about this most of the time since they'd left London and she'd decide for herself about confronting Norris.

Pat urged Deb to be careful, because Chet Norris sounded like a dangerous character.

Deb announced that she could take care of herself. Or else she'd wasted a lot of money and five years on judo and karate lessons.

By this time they'd walked up the slope from the river. In the early twilight they stood outside the glass-walled lobby of the theater where they would see Shakespeare's four-hundred-year-old treacheries, deceits and murders.

Tony looked at Paul Taylor. "Suppose Gary Bonham was paying kickbacks to Chet Norris. Suppose that's why he'd been so quiet, why he'd been drinking so much. Suppose he was working up the nerve to face Norris and cut him off—tell him he wasn't going to pay any more. Think he could do that?"

Taylor glanced ahead to Deb and Pat, who had walked on a few more steps toward the entrance.

"I don't know," he said. "I don't know him as well as you and Deb."

"Make a guess."

Taylor shrugged. At the same time, he moved so that his back was to Deb and Pat. "Based on what I saw at the session yesterday morning? When he stood there like a punching bag and wouldn't defend his agency's work? I'd say no." For a split second Taylor's eyes narrowed. His voice dropped and he said, "Then again, from what I saw at the hotel yesterday afternoon—"

"You saw Gary yesterday afternoon?"

"Yeah. Didn't you know that? At the hotel. Completely different guy from the way he was in the morning. Said he was going to meet Norris, get everything settled, and we'd finish the session. *No problemo,'* he said. That's when he gave me the key."

"He gave you the key? To the studio?"

"Right."

"Why?"

Now confidential and confident, Taylor said, "He said he was meeting Norris there early, gave me the key, said to give it to you, so you could get in."

"That doesn't sound like Gary. Was he sober?"

"Sort of."

"*Sort of!* What does that mean?"

"Sort of sober, sort of not. But he was okay."

"What time was it?"

"How do I know? Three? Three-thirty?" He glanced at his watch and then at the people moving around in the lobby. "We'd better go."

Tony looked away, down toward the arched bridge and the River Avon, dim in the dusk. "So he went to the studio, met Norris, and Norris killed him. Assuming that Norris was there."

"I suppose so. 'Assuming that Norris was there,' as you say."

Pat and Deb still waited, chatting. Now Taylor turned and reached for Deb's arm to go on into the theater. "Now that you mention it," he said over his shoulder to Tony, "where were *you?*"

FOURTEEN

Wednesday—To Oxford and London

EARLY THE NEXT morning Tony and Pat stumbled out of the tall old half-timbered bed-and-breakfast, shuffled across the gravel parking lot, and crawled into their little red rental car.

Pat eased into the seat and let her head tilt back on the headrest. "So that's what the travel folders call 'A Full English Breakfast,'" she said.

Tony burped and turned left onto the narrow road to reverse their trail back to Oxford.

"Eggs and bacon," she went on. "Sausage. Toast with jam and butter. Muffins! If everybody eats that kind of breakfast there isn't an unclogged artery in all of England."

"Beats dry toast and half a grapefruit," he said. "But I don't care for those little racks they use to keep the toast cold." He smiled over at Pat, sitting in the passenger seat with the map on her lap. "Feeling all right?"

"'Yes,' she said with a burp," she said. She sighed a long, deep sigh. "And this was a good idea, getting away from London after that awful experience." She smiled, but kept her eyes on the road ahead. "How about you? Feeling more comfortable with the British way of driving?"

"Oh, yes. 'Piece of cake,' as they say."

"Well, then, before we meet any cars coming from the other direction, it might be a good idea to drive on the right-hand side of the road. They all seem to do it here."

Tony looked ahead. He glanced up to the right, where he always looked for the rear-view mirror, and found the right corner-post. He glanced up to the left, where he usually saw the left corner-post, and found the rear-view mirror. He jerked the car to the right and the tires squeaked across the road. Settled into the proper lane, he said, "It was a test."

"Of course."

"To see how long it would be before you noticed."

"Yes."

The tires hummed on the road's black surface and the sound bounced off the tall hedges along its edge.

"Actually," Tony said, "I was trying to stay away from the curb. These are the only country roads I've seen with little concrete curbs."

Pat reached over and patted him on the knee, in time with her words. "It's all right," she said. "Go back to sleep."

PAUL TAYLOR'S Vauxhall taxi hummed along a broader highway. He and Deb Thomas had stayed at a Stratford inn instead of a back-roads B-and-B, so they were already on the more direct route to Oxford and London.

Deb sat in the swivel chair, swinging back and forth, an exasperated expression on her face. "We had this argument yesterday." She flung her hands up and let them drop in her lap. "The only difference is, yesterday we were going in the other direction."

Taylor raised one finger off the steering wheel and waggled it sideways. "No, no. This is still a conversation. We haven't reached the argument plateau. And all I'm saying is that I agree with Pat Pratt—" He shook his head. "Ridiculous name. I agree with what's-her-name that *you* shouldn't confront Norris with *anything*. I think he can be a very vicious man."

"*You* confronted him."

"Different context. Different game."

"How different?"

"You want to talk to him about his work, about the way he does business, about the way he handles people. Whatever it is, good or bad, it has to do with his job. But. The reason he came after me was different. Even though we were working, it had nothing to do with business.

"He took me on—tried to make me look bad—because he was jealous. The reason he came after me was you."

Deb jerked around to interrupt but he hurried on.

"Let me finish. Please. I think that he knew, maybe sensed, that something had happened between you and me and it ate him up.

"Can't you imagine how he felt? Here he is, trying to marry America's second biggest bakery! And all of a sudden, look who's standing there with frosting on his face. Me! 'The Freak'! With you?—the bakery boss's daughter? He couldn't take that at all.

"So he tried to put me down, tried to make me look bad. And when that didn't work he tried to threaten me. And when that didn't work he started in on everybody else. Bonham. Pratt." He glanced at Deb watching him, listening, rubbing her palms down the crease of her slacks. "And then he started attacking me. Not my work, me. He made it personal, so I finally—well, you heard him, you saw him when he came after me in the lounge and I had to—"

He caught a movement out of the corner of his eyes. "You're shaking your head. You don't believe what I'm saying?"

"I don't know. Maybe what you say about Chet Norris is right. I'm not saying I agree, just 'maybe.' But I'm hearing something else and it confuses me."

"Go."

"You say that if I suspect that he's doing something wrong, that he's mishandling company business, I shouldn't confront him with it."

"Right."

"And the reason I shouldn't confront him is that he might do something to hurt me, one way or another."

"Yes. Very possibly."

"So what you're doing is, you're trying to protect me."

"Yes. Very definitely."

"And yet *you* have been telling *me* not to get 'serious,' quote-unquote, about this relationship of ours."

"Absolutely."

"But if you're trying to protect me, then who's getting 'serious'?"

She waited, till he finally said, "Tilt."

"Don't be funny. Answer me. From what you've said it seems to me that we've got something worth working on. If you agree—if you're gonna be my lover and protector—say so. If not—if I'm just a wham-bam-thank-you-ma'am—say so."

"You are *not* a wham-bam-thank-you-ma'am."

"Good. Then I can put you down as my l-and-p, right?"

"Your what?"

"My lover and protector."

"Right. Temporarily, anyway."

"Don't worry. I'm not asking you to sign a lease, for God's sake."

He held his left hand out. "Deal," he said.

She shook his hand in both of hers. "Deal," she said, and smiled. "You can be a hard man to do business with."

"I'm glad you remember."

She slapped his hand. "Stop that."

They rode for a while with his hand in hers, and then he said, "Back to Chet Norris."

She bobbed her head and sighed. "Yes. But I'm not as sure as you are that he's actually a cruel and vicious person. Greedy, maybe. Maybe crooked. But I'm not sure he's really dangerous."

After a pause he squeezed her hand and said, "I'll tell you something I learned a long time ago, my dear. Believe anything of anyone. Because anyone can be anything."

TONY AND PAT drove back to Oxford, turned in the rented car, and rode the train to London without discussing Bonham's death at all. The only time it was mentioned was when Tony repeated the conversation he'd had with Paul Taylor outside the theater in Stratford. Other than that, nothing.

He tried to bring it up once, on the train, but Pat raised her hand and said, "Please, can we just let it rest?"

They talked about their children, about the trip, about how much additional money they were spending and how much more they'd need if the police made them stay in England longer than they'd planned.

The rest of the time they watched the Thames River Valley slide past the window. Once, after a long silence, Pat stared through Tony's reflection in the window and said, "I wonder how long Paul Taylor and Gary Bonham were together at the hotel?"

LATER THAT AFTERNOON, back in London, Inspector Vincent Pomeroy escorted Tony through his police station like a real estate agent showing a good but slightly rundown piece of income property. Midway along a scuffed narrow hall he stopped at a tall, unframed doorway. "Ah, and here's the canteen," he said, "small but ample. Would you like tea? Coffee?" Suddenly a frown wrinkled all of Pomeroy's round face and he said, "No, not *this* coffee. By this time of the afternoon it's so strong that you can spread it like tar on the roadway. Tea, then? Or something cold?"

"Nothing for me, thank you. But go ahead."

Tony followed Pomeroy into the small rectangle. Along the left wall, two uniformed officers in white shirtsleeves sat at one of three small tables, smoking. They nodded at Pomeroy and inspected Tony.

Vending machines lined the other walls, except for a gap between two, where a waist-high workbench had been inserted to hold a Red Ring coffeemaker, a hot plate with steaming tea kettle, and five crockery mugs upside down on a paper towel in a clutter of sugar packets, stirring sticks and spoons.

Inspector Pomeroy plopped a Littlewood's tea bag into a mug, splashed water over it and sighed, "There. Now let's go on to my little cubicle and have our chat." He sipped at the steaming cup as he walked, but he suddenly stopped and looked at Tony. "You know, of course, the cause of Mr. Bonham's death."

Surprised, Tony said, "No. I don't."

"Oh?" Pomeroy said. "Really." He turned and walked on ahead.

At the end of the hall they turned left into another rectangle, this one lined with three-drawer filing cabinets, some black, some brown, some gray. Several tall bobby helmets rose in stacks on the black cabinet just inside the door. The pale gray walls held no pictures, no plaques, no citations, nothing that usually marks a policeman's office.

In the narrow wall opposite the door, one small window glared in on Pomeroy's black metal desk. He squeezed around the end, steaming mug held high, and eased into his squeaky wooden chair, putting the light behind him.

Tony sat in a straight-back chair on the other side of the desk and looked into the glare at Pomeroy's shadowy face.

"So, Mr. Pratt, you say that you don't know what caused Mr. Bonham's death."

"No. I assumed it was a heart attack or something like that but, no, I don't know how he died. How would I know that?"

Pomeroy paused a few moments, apparently considering Tony's question and deciding not to answer. Instead, he reached out and pulled a file folder across his desk. "The medical report says that the cause of death was—"

Opening the folder, Pomeroy sipped at his tea. "Oh, dear!" he said. "You'd think I'd learn." He lifted the dripping tea bag out of his mug and dropped it into a brown-stained glass ashtray on the corner of his desk. He opened the folder again. "'A severe blow or series of blows to the chest, directly over the heart.'" He sucked up a little more tea as he closed the folder. "And you say you know nothing about that?"

Tony shook his head. "Somebody killed him?"

"So it appears."

"And you think I did it?"

"Seems quite possible."

Tony laughed and the inspector added, "But the situation doesn't seem at all humorous."

"The fact that Gary Bonham is dead isn't funny. What's funny is the idea that I had anything to do with it."

"Why do you say that?"

"Because I wouldn't kill anybody!"

"And why do you say that?"

Tony leaned forward, hands on his knees, arms stiff. He cocked his head a little to the left, a little to the right. "I can't see your face very well but you must be joking."

"As I said, Mr. Pratt, the situation isn't at all humorous. I do not joke about murder." Inspector Pomeroy put the crockery mug down on the corner of his desk and sat with both hands flat on the desktop. He kept his voice calm and even. When he raised it, when he felt it necessary for his voice to carry over Tony's, he raised it only in volume, not intensity. "Now. From our previous conversation I understand that there was quite a little

dust-up in the studio the morning of Mr. Bonham's death.''

''Yes.''

''Mr. Taylor and Mr. Norris spoke quite vigor-
ously to each other, I think you said.''

''Yes, although I doubt that I phrased it quite
that way.''

''More picturesquely, perhaps, but do I have the
sense of it?—that there was a serious disagreement
between Taylor and Norris?''

''Yes.''

''Serious enough that they nearly came to
blows.''

''Yes.''

''And what did you do?''

''What?''

''While all this was going on between Taylor and
Norris, did you not start your own argument with
Mr. Bonham?''

''What?''

The inspector paused, his shadowy head tilted to
one side. ''You are a writer, Mr. Pratt?''

Surprised by the sudden change of topic, Tony
sat up. ''What? Yes.''

''For some reason I always think of writers as
being articulate, even flowery, speakers. But your
vocabulary seems somewhat meager and monosyl-

labic. How can I conduct an intelligent interview if your response is limited to 'yes' and 'what'?"

"What?"

"You see?"

"Gary and I didn't argue."

"Ah. Much better. But I've been led to understand there was a shouting match—"

"Not between Gary and me."

"—that you were so exercised that you jumped to your feet, kicked over a chair—"

"No."

"—charged across the room at Mr. Bonham and came very near to striking him."

"No!" Tony leaned forward and slapped his knees in time with "No, no, no!" He cocked his head again, squinting, trying to see into Pomeroy's shadowed eyes. "I told you what happened. When we talked at the studio, I told you exactly what happened and what you're saying is not it."

"A different view of events, perhaps clearer from another perspective."

"A screwed-up version." Tony turned slightly in the chair. He crossed his legs and hiked his right elbow up to rest on the back of the chair. He settled again, snapped his fingers, and pointed at Pomeroy. "Chet Norris!"

"I beg your pardon?"

"Norris and Eric are the only people you could've talked to. And Eric doesn't have any reason to lie, so he'd tell you straight. But Norris! Norris is the one who had the Class A argument with Paul Taylor. And, indirectly, with Gary Bonham. And Norris threatened Bonham, threatened to pull his account out of Bonham's agency. So..." Tony turned around in the chair again and recrossed his legs. "Norris *does* have a reason to lie, to try to point a finger at someone else. So it's Norris who's been giving you this 'clearer view' that's all screwed up. Right?"

Inspector Pomeroy's answer was to tilt back in his old wooden chair, making it go *screek!* He locked his hands behind his head, elbows pointing wide to the side. His silhouette against the window became a stubby cross. "It's a curious thing, Mr. Pratt, what happens when people are faced with explaining a dead body. They suddenly develop more fingers than toes and they all point away."

Pomeroy tilted forward again and his chair made another racket. He rested his forearms on the desk, one hand stacked on the other on the file folder. "You deny that you came near to blows with Mr. Bonham?"

"Yes."

"Do you deny that you were angry with him?"

"No. I don't deny that. But I didn't kill Gary Bonham."

"We shall see. At the moment it appears that you had the opportunity—"

"When!"

"—during the period in the afternoon that you can't account for, assuming, and I think we'll discover this, that Mr. Bonham returned to the studio during that same period. And it also appears that you may have had the motive, which we will attempt to confirm with further inquiries here and in the States."

The little rectangle of a room was suddenly very quiet. Along the hall from the canteen came a rattle and clunk as someone dropped a coin in a candy machine.

Tony tried to smile but he couldn't make it work. "You're really serious. I'm a suspect in a murder case?"

"I'm afraid so, yes. Everyone connected with the case, as a matter of fact. With the possible exceptions of your wife and Miss Thomas, that is. But I plan to stop by and speak with the others later today. Or am I misremembering?—aren't you scheduled to finish your work today?"

Looking down, shaking his head, Tony rubbed his palms along the creases of his pants. "This is crazy. I couldn't kill anyone."

"Yes, you said that earlier. And why not, may I ask?"

"I just couldn't. I'm just not that sort of person."

"And just what sort of person is 'that sort of person'?"

"Come on, Inspector—"

"Surely, Mr. Pratt, surely by this stage in life you must realize that, given the proper circumstances, we're *all* 'that sort of person.'"

FIFTEEN

Wednesday Afternoon (continued)

TONY WALKED AWAY from Pomeroy's police station shaking his head in disbelief over the inspector's suspicions. But thirty minutes later at the recording studio, when he told his wife about the conversation, Pat's reaction was more vocal.

"He's out of his bloody mind!" She glared across the control room at Tony. Her eyes flicked for a second at the English engineer sitting in front of his control console, who ducked his head between his shoulders like a turtle into its shell. "Pardon me, Eric, but just who the hell do these smug British police think they are, accusing you of—"

"He didn't *accuse* me of—"

"As good as."

"All it is is talk right now, so don't get yourself in a tizzy, as my dear Irish grandmother used to say."

"You never knew your dear Irish grandmother, and it's pretty scary talk coming from a policeman in a foreign country. Right, Eric?"

Eric's head came out and he turned to Pat, shrugging. "I'm not the one to ask. Except for pictures and the telly, this episode is the nearest I've been to a policeman in my entire life."

They all turned toward the open door as Deb Thomas came through and walked up the three steps into the control room. "Me, too. And I'd like to get this job finished and get gone as soon as possible."

"We're all in favor of *that*," Tony said. He picked up two sets of scripts from the stack beside him on the table and stood, handing one set to Deb and looking past her to the door. "Where's Paul? Isn't he with you?"

Deb dropped her bag on the table, took the scripts, and began flipping through the pages as though she'd never seen them before. "I don't know where he is. And no, he isn't with me."

Tony glanced at Pat. She made a face that said "Oh-ho. What happened here?"

Finished with the scripts, Deb rolled them into a tube while she looked around the room. "Why? Isn't he here?"

"Not yet," Tony said.

"Yes, yet." Taylor was standing at the foot of the steps looking up at Deb.

Tony said, "Good. Ready to go?" and tossed Taylor the wrinkled set of marked-up scripts he'd used at the earlier session.

"Always ready. Got to be. Everybody's in such a hurry." He looked up at Deb. "I tried to call you. Thought we'd ride over here together."

She answered as she turned away and pulled out a chair at the table. "I went out. To be by myself."

Taylor frowned at her. "Okay?" She nodded. He looked at Tony. "Okay. Want me in the booth again?"

"Yes. Want to hear the track a couple of times?"

"Nah. Just let me hear the spot we did before."

He went into the isolation booth, sat up on the stool, put the earphones on, and listened to the playback. Then Eric cued up the music track and Taylor recorded the next commercial.

He made one take, they listened to a playback, and Tony turned to Eric. "That's a keeper for me. All right for you?" Eric's head bobbed up and down and Tony asked Deb, "Anything you want to change? Anything you want him to do over?"

"No. Fine." She kept her eyes on the scripts and turned to the next page.

And that's the way it went. Taylor finished the rest of the session in twenty minutes. He didn't say any more to Deb and she didn't even look at him. Except for the words Taylor read, there were only about three other words spoken during those twenty minutes.

When Taylor finished a take, Tony looked around and said, "Okay?" and Eric said, "Good" and Deb said, "Fine."

After Taylor's final take, a re-recording of the spot he'd made Monday, Tony pushed the button on the talk-back mike and said, "That's it, Paul, and thank you very much. Now if you could just sit there for a minute or so, we'll tape a little room tone."

Taylor nodded, crossed his arms and slumped on the stool, sitting quietly. Eric turned on the big tape machine again, hit RECORD, punched another button and said, "Room tone."

Deb looked at Tony and raised her eyebrows, questioning.

"Recording the sound of the room. 'Ambient sound,' as they say. Every studio, every microphone has a little different sound every day—temperature, humidity, whatever. So if, by any chance, we have to edit anything on these tapes, we can fill any little holes in the background with the sound of this room on this day."

At that moment the phone by Eric's console rang with its distinctive British *brip-brip*. Eric, standing by one of his tape machines, almost leaned across the room and snatched up the phone to cut off its high-pitched double ring.

"Eric here! I thought I left strict orders not to ring during—"

He stopped to listen for a moment, apparently overpowered by the telephone's buzzing voice.

"*Bzbzbzz.*"

"I see."

"*Bzbzz?*"

"Just finished."

"*Bzz.*"

"Yes, sir."

Eric carefully returned the phone to its cradle and said to Tony, "Detective Inspector Pomeroy is on his way back."

POMEROY STEPPED UP into the control room just as Tony finished giving Eric instructions on shipping duplicates of the tapes to Abe Arthur at the agency in San Francisco. Then, with the monitors turned off, the big silver reels revolved slowly, the volume needles jumped madly in time with unheard music and voices, and the machines silently made the copies while the inspector once again revived the dead Gary Bonham.

Paul Taylor, seeming bored with Pomeroy's questions, said once more that he'd talked with Bonham at the hotel bar on Monday afternoon;

that Bonham had something he wanted to give to Deb Thomas, some kind of evidence that Chet Norris was doing something illegal, taking kickbacks or something; that he, Taylor, had told Bonham not to get Deb involved, because it might be dangerous for her. "I told him to take whatever he had direct to Deb's father. Or to the law."

For the first time that afternoon, Deb Thomas watched Paul Taylor. Her eyes never left his face while he talked. She seemed not to blink or breathe until he stopped.

And when Inspector Pomeroy spoke to Deb, she turned the same stare on him and told him that the last time she'd spoken to Gary Bonham had been Monday afternoon. Midafternoon. She didn't remember the time.

"He said that he was calling from the lobby. He sounded as though he'd been drinking. He said he had evidence against Chet Norris and he wanted me to take it to my father. He said Chet was taking kickbacks from the agency and from other suppliers. He said Chet wanted more money, and if he didn't get it he'd take our account away from Gary's agency. Gary said he'd recorded the conversation and he wanted to give me the tape."

Pomeroy's eyes flickered and Tony sat up and they both said, almost simultaneously, "A tape?"

Deb said, "That's what he said. And he wanted me to take it to my father."

Pomeroy leaned forward. "Miss Thomas, why didn't you mention this before?"

She sat with her eyes down, fixed on her hands clenched in her lap. "I told you. Just now." She raised her head, staring straight at Paul Taylor while she talked to Pomeroy. "He'd been drinking. I thought that he'd had too much to drink and that he might be fabricating something about Chet Norris because Chet had humiliated him earlier, at the studio."

The inspector started to speak but Pat cut in and said to Tony, "Suppose Gary Bonham *did* have a tape. Of a conversation like that. And suppose he met Norris here, confronted him with the tape, and threatened to take it to his boss. Would Norris kill him because of that?"

Tony shrugged. "It's possible."

Pomeroy sounded much more assertive. "It's *quite* possible."

"Bullshit!" Chet Norris almost shouted from the foot of the steps. "With all due respect, Inspector, you're out of your mind."

Inspector Pomeroy rose and started toward the door. "Mr. Norris, perhaps we could—"

Norris cut him off. "I don't know anything about kickbacks or tapes or meeting Bonham here or any of this other bullshit you've been kicking around in here."

Pomeroy continued slowly down the steps. "If you wouldn't mind, sir—"

Looking past the inspector, Norris ignored him and said loudly, "The only reason I'm here, Deb, is to tell you personally that I called your father and he expects you to follow through with me on these distributor meetings."

Pomeroy stepped down off the bottom step and stood almost nose to nose with the American. "Mr. Norris," he said, as Norris started to back away, and Deb called out, "Chet, wait a minute!"

"That's all, Deb!" He continued backing down the corridor. "I expect to see you in the hotel lobby tomorrow morning at six-thirty, ready to catch the train to Manchester." He turned and stalked down the corridor.

Following behind, Pomeroy said, "Believe me, Mr. Norris, you would do better to stop and talk to me."

Norris didn't stop. Over his shoulder he said, "I've already told you, Inspector. I didn't kill Gary Bonham. I don't know anything about kickbacks. I don't know anything about tapes. I don't know anything about anything so I don't have anything to talk to you *about*."

He stopped so suddenly that Pomeroy almost bumped into him. Without turning around he said, "So unless you're going to arrest me, Inspector, get off my ass."

He crossed the lobby and shoved the front door open as Deb and Tony caught up with Pomeroy and they all rushed after him, through the door and out onto the sidewalk. Cabs, cars, and trucks roaring by in the busy street made so much noise that Pomeroy had to shout. "Mr. Norris!"

Again Norris ignored the inspector. He signaled a taxi driver parked at the cab stand across the street and without a pause stepped between two cars parked at the curb.

Instantly Pomeroy saw what was about to happen. He shouted again. "Norris! Stop!"

Norris paid no attention. Looking carefully to his left he didn't even see the truck that came from the right and crushed him into the street.

SIXTEEN

Friday Afternoon—Musket Beach,
Oregon

PAT HAD HER favorite spot on the beach all to herself. It was in the sheltering curve of a giant piece of driftwood, the widespread base and thick trunk of an old, old cedar. She discovered it four years ago, on the morning after it washed ashore during one of the wildest winter storms Musket Beach had ever known. The thing probably weighed a ton, she thought, but the brutal sea carried it in and dropped it on the beach like an albatross feather.

One day the sea would carry it away again, but now the silvery old cedar half-buried in the sand was Pat's favorite place on the beach. Tucked into the curve where its wide base curled into the tapering trunk, she found protection from the wind and a perfect shoulder to rest her head on. Sometimes, sitting beside it, reading, Pat would absently reach out to slide her palm along the wood, feeling it, smooth as bone, warm as flesh in the sun.

Now, relaxed on the sand with her knees drawn up and her toes digging in, she leaned back against her log and closed her eyes.

Tony had been right, she thought. The place to fight jet lag was here on the Oregon coast. "We'll just go to the beach," he'd said, "sit down, and wait for our brains to catch up with our bodies."

So, red-eyed and punchy after their long night flight from London, they'd semi-staggered through Portland International, stopped at their house in suburban Lakewood only long enough to do a load of laundry and call the kids at college, and headed straight for their cabin at Musket Beach.

Once here, he'd dropped onto the couch and almost immediately started making sleeping noises. With her eyes closed, Pat smiled to herself at the memory of one of the kids, Dan or Jenny, much younger, waddling into the kitchen to tell her "Daddy's on the couch, making sleeping noises."

Suddenly Pat's eyes snapped open. She jerked up, rigid, scared, looking across the beach, searching for something in the gentle surf, in the white curls turning to foam along the ocean's edge. She squeezed her eyes shut and let her head droop on her chest. She dug both hands into the sand at her sides, hard. She squeezed her buried hands into fists and felt the grit pile up under her fingernails. She slid her hands out of the sand and opened her eyes as she opened her hands and watched the sand fall into two small piles.

Repeating the word had brought it back. "Noises." "Noises" became "sounds" and Pat remembered opening the door and hearing the sickening crunch as Gary Bonham fell face down at her feet. She shivered, and in her mind the truck screeched and Chet Norris screamed as it smashed him into the street.

Pat shivered again, remembering Inspector Pomeroy.

JUST A FEW HOURS after seeing Norris die in the street fifty yards away, he'd sat across from Pat and Tony in a Soho pub and calmly munched fish and chips. Wiping greasy fingers on a greasy paper napkin, Pomeroy had said, "It's over. Finished." He'd tried to speak lightly but he couldn't hide the bitter undertone in his voice. "Word has come down from on high. Those much wiser than I have said: 'Case closed.'"

He rolled the dirty napkin into a ball and dropped it on his plate. "So. As far as the department is concerned, you may all go on about your business. If that means back to the States, so be it."

They'd studied him for a long moment before Tony said, "Are you telling us that you know who killed Gary Bonham?"

"Mm-hmm. Yes, sir." Pomeroy nodded and drank some of his dark brown ale. "Mr. Norris," he said, and drank some more.

"Norris?"

Pomeroy put the tall glass on the table and said, "We believe that Mr. Norris had motive. That is, that Mr. Bonham had threatened to disclose certain information to Mr. Norris's employer, the president of Thomas Baking Company, who also happens to be the father of Miss Deborah Thomas. Disclosure of this information, having to do with Norris's 'shakedown' tactics, as I believe you call it, would almost surely result in Mr. Norris's immediate dismissal from a fairly prestigious and very well-paid position.

"We believe that Mr. Norris had the opportunity to commit the crime when Mr. Bonham confronted him with his disclosure threat at the studio on Monday afternoon just before your work was to resume.

"We believe that there was an altercation, that Mr. Norris struck Mr. Bonham heavily and repeatedly in the chest over the heart, the blows resulting in Mr. Bonham's death. He had been drinking quite excessively, had Mr. Bonham, and was unable to defend himself. The drink quite likely, along with his already tense emotions, contributed to the effect of the blows to his heart."

With the back of one hand Pomeroy shoved his empty plate toward the edge of the table while he signaled to a waiter with the other. Tony and Pat stared down into their teacups.

"Well," Pomeroy said with surprise in his voice. "Well, why the sudden distressed silence?"

Pat looked at him and said, "I am not in the habit of quarreling with London's Metropolitan Police, but that seems to me a somewhat 'iffy' solution."

"*If* they met at the studio," Tony said, "*if* they were alone, *if* they had a fight, and on and on and—"

"*Somebody* struck him," Pomeroy interrupted, "repeatedly and hard."

"What about Taylor?" Tony asked.

"What about you?" Pomeroy watched Tony, and Pat watched Pomeroy, shocked.

"I was being serious," Tony said.

"As I was."

Tony ignored that comment and said, "Taylor may be small but he's strong as a bull."

Pat said, "You saw what happened, in the lounge, when he hit Norris."

"As for his motive," Tony went on, "he could have been protecting Deb Thomas."

"As for *your* motive," the inspector persisted, "I understand that you were quite upset with Bonham for not protecting your interests?—when Norris threw you off his account and threatened to expose your 'incompetence' to other clients?''

Pat slumped back in her chair, her body language as scornful as her voice. "Really, Inspector."

His eyes shifted from Tony to Pat and back again. "All right, let's leave the Americans out of it entirely, shall we?" He leaned forward on his elbows. "We are in Soho, remember. So let us suppose that one of these street animals sees a wealthy-looking American strolling along Dean Lane and decides to cosh him. Your Mr. Bonham, as it happens. The animal follows him. He turns into a building. The animal follows. No one else around. He bashes Norris and drags him inside the nearly dark studio. But before he can snatch the wallet and the watch and the other little lollies, someone begins to fiddle the door at the far end of the studio. He stuffs the body behind the fake door and sneaks out as Mrs. Pratt comes in, and the rest we know."

There had been a long silence in the pub after that speculation by Pomeroy, and then Tony'd shrugged and said, "That solution is just as plausible as the other."

"Frankly, Inspector," Pat added, "*that* solution is no less 'iffy' than the original."

Inspector Pomeroy sighed a deep sigh. "That may be. That may be. And frankly, Mrs. Pratt, Mr. Pratt—unless there's been a rock-solid witness, every murder case from the dawn of time has had an 'iffy' solution." He picked up the check with one hand and pulled out his wallet with the other. "But in this case the department is satisfied that we have more than plausibly matched victim to motive to method to perpetrator. It's over. The file is closed, as far as we are concerned." He tugged a five-pound note from his wallet and smiled for the first time since they'd met him. "So forget all about it and go back to the States, remembering only that the Metropolitan Police stood you to watercress sandwiches and tea."

LEANING BACK against her log again, Pat closed her eyes. "We came back," she said to herself, "but it's damned hard to forget."

Then, before she heard his voice or saw his shadow cross her closed eyelids, she knew Tony was there. "You're frowning," he said. "Is that the way to treat a beautiful day?"

She opened one eye, squinting up at him. "At least I wasn't snoring."

"Neither was I."

"In the cabin? On the couch? Sounded like snoring to me."

"It's one of my trick sounds."

"Oh?"

"When I use it at home, you put dinner on the table. When I use it at the cabin, you come down here and sit by your log."

"Remarkable. I would swear you were snoring."

"That's why it's such a good trick."

"Do you have any others?"

"One. I'm saving it for tonight."

"Oh-ho."

"Meanwhile, how about a walk?"

"Good idea."

She held out her hands and he pulled her to her feet. "Thought we might go down to Kilchis Point," he said, "see if the cormorants are still around." He watched her slapping the sand off the seat of her jeans. "Want some help with that?"

"Not in public."

She grabbed his shoulder to use him as a prop while she worked her sneakers off with her toes. "There," she said. And with Tony carrying her shoes, they walked down to the firmer sand at the ocean's edge, turned left and started toward the point.

Kilchis Point, jutting into the ocean about a half-mile ahead, marked the southern end of the shallow curve of sand called Musket Beach. Mount

Kenai, about a half-mile behind them with the town of Musket Beach resting at its foot, marked the northern end.

Oregon's north coast was draped with a string of such coves, and the tip of each cove had a tall, bold outcropping of stone standing in the sea. Behind and below the stone the coastline fell away to the south and gave way slowly to the sea, as witnessed by the curve of sandy beach. Then at the end of the arc the land rose again and there stood another wall of stone with the constant sea rushing at its feet.

Between the tips the coastline was, for the most part, mudstone and sandstone. The tips were mostly basalt. The basalt once flowed as molten lava from ancient volcanoes erupting under the sea or inland. The lava cooled and stood fast against the insistent ocean, while the softer coastline slowly washed away.

At low tide Tony and Pat often walked around the headlands and points from one cove to the next, from one beach to another, mile after mile. Once they'd even considered the possibility of walking down the Oregon coast all the way to California, from the Columbia River to the California line.

But that had been late on a fine fall evening after Tony received a very fine check from his publisher and they'd enjoyed several particularly fine drinks before an unusually fine dinner and a remarkably fine wine followed by some extraordinarily fine Drambuie.

They had no such thoughts in their heads now. They walked silently arm in arm beside the roll and surge of the surf, barely aware of the five or six other people on the beach. Pat turned her head now and then to search for pelicans gliding over the ocean swells. Tony watched about thirty sanderlings scurry ahead of them over the wet sand, running so fast their legs disappeared in a blur. Suddenly, with a rush as if a giant hand had tossed them all in the air, they were up and flying, flashing their white wingbars as they banked right and then left over the surf.

And just as suddenly Tony said, "It was Paul Taylor. Taylor killed Gary."

Pat reached up and rubbed the back of his neck through his sweatshirt. "I thought that's what you were thinking about."

"Trying to keep him away from Deborah Thomas. To protect her."

Pat slid her hand down to his elbow, tugged, and they both stopped. "Would you repeat that?"

He put his arm around her waist and they started walking again. "Bonham said that Norris was a crook, that he used his position with Thomas Baking to shake down suppliers. Bonham said he had some kind of evidence against Norris. He wanted

Deb to take it to her father. But Taylor didn't want that. He wanted to keep Deb out of it. He knew what a mean bastard Norris could be, so he wanted Bonham to bypass Deb and go straight to her old man. Or to the police. But Bonham said no. Maybe he thought that Deb would have more of an impact on her dad, make him move faster. Anyway, Taylor and Bonham argued about it and Taylor got pretty fired up—we've all seen him get pretty physical. So he punches Bonham, Bonham drops, and that's that.''

" 'That's that'?'' Pat shook her head as if confused. ''Where did 'that' happen?''

''The studio. Where else?''

''Why in the world would those two be at the studio together?''

''I don't know. Yet.''

Pat looked down, for a few steps dragging her toes through the sand.

''Well,'' she said, shielding her eyes from the glare on the water. ''Well.'' They were much closer to Kilchis Point, now, and she studied the two great rocks standing in the ocean about a hundred yards off the point. ''Till then, you had a very tidy theory working.'' The rocks, two hundred feet tall and nearly that wide, provided nesting and hunting grounds for hundreds of birds. She watched a pair of gulls gliding gracefully above the rocks. The birds seemed to hang in the air, white wings wide and playing with the wind. "However—"

Tony nodded. "Right. 'A very tidy theory. However.'"

She answered him with another nod and started to go on but then interrupted herself, pointing at the rocks. "Look! Cormorants!"

Three large black birds—long necks, arched backs, rapid wingbeats—whipped over the water below the gulls. They flew toward the tall rock on the left, angled up its side and then, wings held wide, hung in the air for a moment perpendicular to the rock face before they landed by their nests.

"I was about to say," Pat went on, "I don't mean to sound negative. However. As I recall, Deb Thomas and Paul Taylor were having some kind of 'lover's quarrel' about that time. So I'm not so sure that either one felt particularly 'protective' toward the other."

Tony shook his head. "They came to the studio together, and they went to Stratford together."

"You may not have noticed it. At Stratford, for example. Except for the play itself, did you notice that she spent more time talking to me than to Taylor? And as far as 'protection' is concerned, remember what she said about taking judo and karate lessons for, what, five years? I would say that Deb Thomas is a woman who definitely doesn't need protection. Emotionally, physically, whatever. Oh, we all want to feel that way, to some degree, but—''

Pat smiled and looped an arm around Tony's waist. "Maybe *you're* the one who needs protecting, my dear, because you always seem to think that *women* need protecting." She stopped and the smile slowly faded and she frowned, looking at the rocks and then at Tony. "Actually, it could have been a woman who did it.''

They'd reached Kilchis Point now, and Pat slowly turned to look at the sea and the surf and the birds in front of them, at the stone cliff leading up to the fir- and cedar-covered slopes of Kilchis Point State Park behind them.

She sighed and said, "I guess I *do* sound negative. I don't mean to. I guess if we were walking along here talking about one of your stories, I'd feel differently. But it's a beautiful day and—I'm sorry—but I hate to be walking on the beach on a beautiful day with dead bodies as the topic of conversation. *Real* dead bodies, not something in a novel. So please. Inspector Pomeroy said the case is closed. Can we leave it that way? Please?"

SEVENTEEN

Saturday Morning—Musket Beach

PAUL TAYLOR HAD built a small masterpiece of a house on the side of Mount Kenai. His view of the beach and the ocean could easily be the opening shot of a movie.

In the foreground about a half-mile down the slope would be the town of Musket Beach with its shingled roofs clustered along the ocean shore. Opening the camera lens and panning up a little would put the town across the bottom of the frame in a wide-angle shot and beyond the town the deep blue Pacific Ocean would swell and roll away till the swells and lazy whitecaps disappeared over the horizon in a haze, a haze so far away that it might be infinity or it might be smog over Honolulu. The top third of the picture would be white, flat-bottomed clouds in a sunny sky.

Along the left edge of the frame, the Oregon coastline would stretch about as far south as Tony and Pat had planned to walk. That is, almost to California.

To see Taylor's back yard the camera would have to swing one-hundred-eighty degrees, change focus, tilt up, and there would be the mountainside climbing almost a thousand fir-covered feet to Mount Kenai's round top.

Taylor had found the site several years ago when he was taking a few weeks of vacation. In Malibu, he and his fourth wife had jumped into his first Rolls-Royce for a drive north. Just "north." He was looking for a hideaway, a place where he could go to separate himself from the Hollywood hassle. When he got to Oregon he knew he was getting close, and when he saw Musket Beach he knew he'd found it.

So he bought this beautiful site and built this beautiful small house. His house looked as though it had been planted, had grown and been carefully pruned, and now seemed as natural to the mountainside as a huckleberry bush. Looking at it, no one would know that one of the rooms was a small recording studio, so that he could do some of his work here and not in Hollywood.

His fourth wife liked the idea. She thought that if he spent less time in Hollywood he'd be less likely to stray. She knew how easily Taylor's galloping hormones tripped and fell among the temptations that Southern California laid in their path. Having been, herself, one of those temptations.

What she didn't understand was that Northern Oregon had hormones of its own. She also didn't understand, or perhaps didn't admit, a certain basic physiological fact about her husband. He was attuned to women. If Paul Taylor were set down in the middle of the Gobi Desert, he would sense, instantly, the presence of any female within five hundred miles. She might be a camel, but he would find a way to send flowers and wine.

So, even in tiny Musket Beach, Oregon, Taylor found his hormones of the month. They steamed through the pipes of the young wife of the aging real estate agent who sold the land to Taylor.

Both the young wife and the old husband later turned up dead—Taylor wasn't involved in either death; his only guilt was glandular—but the affair turned Taylor's fourth wife into his fourth ex-wife and made his name well known in Musket Beach. His reputation increased when the gossipy locals passed the word about his divorce settlement: his wife could have the Malibu house *if* he got to keep the house in Musket Beach.

Never one to knock a little notoriety, he added to it by buzzing the town in his Cessna every time he flew in from Los Angeles.

"You fly, too?"

When Deborah Thomas asked the question early that Saturday morning, it didn't sound like a question but more like a statement. It came through the telephone flat and uninflected, as though she'd aimed it from Chicago straight at Musket Beach and wanted no interference from mountains, canyons, rivers or large rocks.

"Yeah," he said. "Makes it simpler when I have to go to L.A.," Taylor answered. "Simpler getting back, too." He'd taken her call in his kitchen, and while he talked he looked around to see if his coffeemaker had finished its job.

"Musket Beach has an airport?"

"No." Trailing the long telephone cord behind him, he circled the kitchen, opening and closing the refrigerator and several cabinet doors. "A town called Seashore Village, about fifteen minutes north. There's an airstrip there." He paused. "But there's no bread here."

"What does that have to do with anything?" She sounded cold and lifeless.

He laughed. "I wanted to make some toast. It's six-thirty in the morning where I'm standing."

"Oh."

"I haven't even had any coffee." No response. He frowned but kept his voice animated. "So anyway, as I was saying, let me know when you're coming in. I'll fly over to Portland, meet you at the airport. Okay?"

"We have to talk." She sounded cold and life-less. "About us."

"You said that."

"And about the other thing."

"You said that, too." His eyes rolled up in his head but he sounded loose, relaxed. "Tell me your schedule again."

Pouring a cup of coffee, he heard her flipping through her appointment book and muttering. "Tough schedule. Ten days of meetings on the coast. San Diego to Los Angeles to San Francisco, then Portland and Seattle. Let's see. I can fly up from San Fran on Friday afternoon for my Portland meetings on Monday morning."

"Good," he said, warm and excited. "I'll be there when you walk off the plane. Just be sure you've got carry-on bags and we'll be in and out of that airport before you know it. Then we'll fly back here and I'll treat you to a weekend at the Oregon coast. You'll love it."

"We've got to talk."

"We'll talk, we'll talk. If you want to, we'll talk till it runs out your—"

He stopped to shut off his irritation, then put a smile in his voice and said, "Hey, lighten up. Where's my London lady?"

"I don't know. I feel so different since I got back. There was a lot of excitement pumping over there, but when I got home it all drained away. Now all I do is think about what happened. And worry.''

''Don't think about it. Don't worry. Just let me know your flight time and I'll meet—''

''Friday, four-fifty-five, United.''

He laughed. ''Great. Can't wait. I'll see you Friday and fly you away to Musket Beach.''

''That'll be good,'' she said, beginning to sound comfortable for the first time. ''I think I'm looking forward to it. And we can—''

''Right. We can talk.''

THERE'S ONLY ONE place in Musket Beach where the locals show up early on Saturday morning. The bakery.

Any other day, Monday through Friday, they can walk in just about any old time and find what they're looking for. On Saturday, though, the tourists are in town. Therefore, the locals get to the bakery early, before the tourists snatch up every cinnamon roll, caramel roll, doughnut, Danish, popover, turnover and loaf of bread in sight.

That's why Pat Pratt was among the eight or nine people standing outside the bakery's big bay window three minutes before the door opened at eight o'clock. Pat was in line behind Maggie Margolis, owner of the Musket Beach Book Store. As usual, Maggie fired off a string of questions at Pat, such things as when would Tony's next mystery novel be out—"Some time in the spring," Pat said—and how did she like the trip to England—"Quite interesting, quite unusual"—and did Tony plan to use the trip as background for a book—"Most likely."

A male voice broke in. "He'd be a fool if he didn't." Pat and Maggie turned around and found Paul Taylor standing beside them. Taylor shifted down to his deep, rolling, announcerish voice. "Untold possibilities lie in that journey."

"Well, speaking of England," Pat said, "Maggie, do you know Paul Taylor?"

"Only by reputation," she said, and walked away into the just-opened bakery.

Surprised, Taylor looked at Maggie's back and then at Pat. "Never saw her before in my life."

"I think she's connecting you to the late mayor. Or his wife."

"Ah, yes. 'The recent unpleasantness.'" Taylor spoke as if he were reading a script. "'The real estate agent and his wife. A tale best forgotten.'" Although he was about half-a-head shorter than Pat, he took her elbow and escorted her into the bakery. "Whatever it was, it's history. On to the present and in to the goodies. I'm glad we ran into each other. I've just heard from another member of our jolly old England group."

"Oh, really." Pat stopped in the middle of the bakery while the other customers flowed around them like a wave around a rock.

"Deb Thomas. She's coming out to the coast on business and she'll be here next weekend."

"Here? In Musket Beach?"

"The very same. And I'd like to invite you and Tony to join us for lunch at my place next Saturday."

"Well, how interesting."

"'Interesting,'" Taylor said. "Does that translate to 'yes' or 'no' or 'I'll talk it over with Tony' or—"

"I'm sorry. Yes. Lunch on Saturday. I was distracted because Tony and I were just talking about you. Again."

"Again?"

Pat nodded. "He was telling me an interesting theory he has about you and Chet Norris."

Taylor studied Pat with the most serious expression she'd seen on his face that morning. "Tony has a theory about me? And Chet Norris? Maybe Tony and I should get together. Have a drink or two. A little chat."

"Good idea," Pat said. "Maybe it'd clear things up."

EIGHTEEN

Saturday Afternoon—Musket Beach

TONY AND TAYLOR met for the drink and the chat, but the only thing it cleared up was Tony's determination.

They met at BDS, a bar made out of a beach-front cabin next door to the Sea & Sand Motel. The coasters and napkins and the wood sign out front said BUCKLEY'S SALOON, but Buckley kept the place so dark that somebody started calling it Buckley's Dark Saloon, somebody else cut that to BDS, and before long that's what everybody called it.

An attractive young waitress took them to a wooden booth in the corner, away from the crowd jammed around the little tables by the front windows and stacked along the bar. Sliding into the booth Tony said, "Just coffee" and Taylor told the waitress, "Coffee for my father, with a splash of Metamucil. I'll have a double Tanqueray gin over ice. With a twist. Water back."

The waitress turned and Taylor watched her walk away while he said to Tony, "So. Your wife mentioned some kind of 'interesting theory' you've worked out, some kind of scenario about what happened in London. Something to do with Chet Norris and me. The *late* Chet Norris."

"Conjectures, that's all," Tony said. "I wouldn't say I've got a scenario, yet. More of a 'story treatment,' maybe."

Taylor shrugged. "Whatever. I'd like to hear it. The sorry truth is," he looked up at the waitress as she came back with their drinks, "I'm a sucker for any story that has me in it, good or bad. How 'bout you?"

"Oh, I'm good," she said. "And bad." She handed him the check and left.

Swirling the lemon peel around in his drink, he watched her walking away again. "I dearly love lumpy young ladies like that," he murmured. "I truly do."

Tony smiled a little, watching Taylor watching the girl till she disappeared around the end of the bar.

Taylor bit the end off his lemon twist and turned back to Tony, chewing. "So, as we were saying, your 'story treatment,' if you don't mind—" He raised his glass to Tony and then sipped.

"No, I don't mind. *You* might, though."

"Nah," Taylor laughed, "I just told you. Any story with me in it is all right. So go."

"Okay. What I see is, Gary Bonham's in the hotel bar Monday afternoon. This is after the session blew up Monday morning. He's trying to work out a problem that's been bothering him, so he's in the bar drinking and thinking.

"Something you should know is that this isn't new to Gary. He's tried it before and it never works. He could think or he could drink. He just couldn't do both at the same time. But he never understood that. So by the time he gets half stoned he thinks he's solved the problem. But he hasn't. All he's got is drunk.

"Anyway, Gary's problem *this* time, as he sees it, is to get rid of Chet Norris but to keep the Thomas Baking Company as a client. Thomas Baking is his client, not Chet Norris. So he has to get Chet Norris fired and still hang on to the company.

"Now, how can he do that? He, the outside agency, can't complain to his client's management because Norris was recently appointed Marketing Director and sits on the management committee. So the action against Norris has to come from inside the company.

"That's when a great big bulb lights up over Gary's head and guess who's standing there in the glow?—Deborah Thomas. Deb's family not only owns the bakery, her father is the president. Talk about *inside*.

"So Gary staggers, stumbles, falls out of the bar to find Deb to get her help. But he finds you, first. He tells you his plan, knowing that there's something going on between you and Deb—Gary may have been wimpy but he wasn't a dummy.

"You tell him to leave Deb out of it. 'Screw you,' he says, in effect, and tries to call Deb. She's not in her room, so he leaves a message asking her to meet him at the studio. You overhear it. And you hear him leave the same message for Norris. And when he starts to take off for the studio you try to stop him, try to keep him away from Deb.

"He won't be stopped, though. He's a pretty big guy and he's loaded and you don't want a big scene there in the hotel, but you can't think of a way to stop him. He's determined to get to the studio.

"So maybe you drive him there in your taxicab. Or maybe you follow him when he leaves the hotel. One way or the other you catch up with him at the studio and you tell him again, 'Leave Deb out of it!' and he tells you that this is agency-client business, no outsiders allowed.

"That, by the way, is something else you should know about Gary. It was one of his favorite ideas, one of the few things he felt strongly about. 'The sanctity of the agency-client relationship,' he called it. He almost made it sound holy." Tony shook his head. "But *he* took it seriously. In fact, I've seen him get very emotional about it."

Taylor shrugged. "I wouldn't know. Go ahead."

"So you're at the studio, you and Gary, arguing. You're still trying to protect Deb and he's still trying to do something that he thinks will protect his company. He loses his temper. So do you.

"The difference is, when Gary gets mad, all he does is yell, whereas you—with that muscleman torso you've developed—you punch.

"Remember what that bobby said when you coldcocked Norris? 'Never seen a man hit so bloody hard in my life.' And that's how you hit Gary, despite the fact that he's well over a head taller than you. You pound him. Once, twice, who knows, three times—hard—in the chest, right over his heart.

"Bonham drops. The key to the studio falls out of his hand, the key I'd given him. You pick it up, drag his body into the studio, shove it behind the sound effects door, and sneak out just as Pat comes in.

"You hustle out and go back to the hotel and, my guess is, you run into Deb on her way to meet Bonham. You drive her back to the studio and let yourselves in with the key that fell out of his hand when you hit him. And that's how you got the key you dropped in my hand later that night."

The two men were quiet after Tony finished, and then Taylor picked up his glass and drained his drink. He held his head back with the glass over his mouth and jiggled the glass until a piece of ice slid into his mouth. He put down his glass and nodded. "Clever thinking," he said, chewing the ice. "And it's not every day I get accused of murder." He let out a short laugh and tossed his head as he wiped shimmering drops of gin and ice water off his beard with the back of his hand. "It only seems to happen when I get mixed up with you and your wife."

Taylor slid across the booth, about to leave. He pulled a sheaf of money-clipped bills out of his pocket, snapped off a five, and dropped it on the table. "However clever it is, though, all you have is a rough story line. Not a scenario. Not even a 'treatment,' as you called it."

"No, what I said was that I'd made some 'conjectures.' And I'll admit that I'm forgetting something, but it'll come back and—"

Taylor cut in and his voice was flat and hard. "And I'll tell you what it is you've got. Call it conjectures, speculation, theory, whatever you wanta call it—"

"I think it's pretty close to the way it happened, Paul."

"And I say it's Bull. Shit. There was only one word in all that talk that really counted. 'Guess.' That's all you've got there, a long string of guesses. Bull. Shit. In a tall pile."

Tony edged forward and started to say something when Taylor suddenly smiled, leaned back against the back of the booth, and spread his arms wide in a magnanimous gesture. "But, hey. What the hell difference does it make? Suppose I *did* punch Bonham and suppose he *did* drop dead—although you'd have a hard time explaining why I'd knock off one of *my* biggest clients—suppose I did it. Now what? It was in England. In a foreign country. And the cops there have closed the case. Right? There's not one, single, bloody, flaming thing anybody can do about it. Right?"

Watching Taylor's performance, and he was sure that's what it was, Tony's answer was a slight shrug and tilt of the head.

Taylor could've read the gesture as a sign of agreement or he could've read it as Tony saying no, there's something *I* can do about it.

Taylor took it for agreement and answered his own question. "Right." He grinned and let his voice fall in a country accent. "Ain't nothin' nobody kin do."

He eased out of the booth and stood up. "'Cept enjoy ourself at the beach." He dropped a heavy hand on Tony's shoulder and smiled a big, good-ole-boy smile. "You have an outstanding day now, y'hear? And don't you worry nothin' 'bout—"

He stopped. His head jerked up as if he'd heard someone call his name. At that instant the waitress appeared beside him.

"Everything all right?" she smiled.

"I-deal," he smiled back. "My pappy was just leavin'."

NINETEEN

Saturday Evening—Musket Beach

THE SUN SEEMED to be melting on the horizon. All that remained was the top third, bulging at the sides and going fast, a river of liquid gold overflowing its banks and spreading over the flat plain of the sea.

Above the white ribbon of surf three gulls floated through the air, in silhouette as black as crooked-wing crows.

Swallows darted through the last sunlight, feeding, searching the air over the street and the cabin.

Tony carried two glasses of white wine through the open door of the cabin and out to the deck. He handed one glass to Pat, who sat relaxed in a low lounge chair with her legs stretched out and her crossed bare feet resting on the lower railing of the deck.

"Look," she said, pointing up. "Barn swallows. Look at the wings, so shiny and so blue in this light. No black at all. And the breast. As orange as a robin's."

"Beautiful." Tony stood beside her chair, quiet, watching the rim of the sun disappear but leave behind a thin evening light. He listened to the surf and the birds and looked up at a bright three-quarter moon. "Beautiful evening."

After another silence he said,

"Look how the pale Queen of the silent night
Doth cause the Ocean to attend upon her.
And he, as long as she is in his sight,
With his full tide is ready for her honor."

Pat raised her glass in salute. "Very nice. Is that something you've been working on?"

"Oh, no. It's more than three hundred years old."

"Really? Who wrote it?"

"Damned if I know. I saw it in a book of quotations this morning. Put it in my temporary memory just for you."

"Well, thank you," she said. "That's somewhat romantic." She smiled and raised her glass again. "And I'll sip to that."

After the toast, Tony hoisted himself up on the deck railing. "Now," he said, but Pat interrupted with a heavy sigh.

"Well, at least we got through dinner without talking about it." She shifted around in her chair. "Okay. Now you want to switch the talk from 'somewhat romantic' to talk about dead bodies. And I guess I've put it off long enough.''

He started to speak but she cut in again. ''But tell me something, first. Why are you so wound up with this thing? The police don't care any more! Inspector Pomeroy said the case was closed. Why keep picking at it?''

''Because Inspector Pomeroy is wrong. Flat wrong. And if I'm right, Bonham was killed by one of four people. One of whom could be me.''

''No.''

''Good. Number Two could be Chet Norris. He's dead, so I'm not worried about him. Three and Four are Paul Taylor and/or Deb Thomas.''

Tony swung around and put both feet on the deck, leaning back against the rail. ''Them I worry about. Paul Taylor is right here in Musket Beach right now. Deb Thomas will be here next weekend. I don't want us to be that close to a killer.''

Pat looked away for a moment. ''Never thought of it that way. To me, it's something that's still 'over there.' In London.'' She turned back and looked up at Tony. ''But it's here?''

''Yes.''

''But what *about* Chet Norris. *Could* Norris have done it?''

"I doubt it. Not one-hundred percent 'no,' but I doubt it. I don't think he had the guts or the strength to do something like that."

"Really? I got the impression that he was a pretty strong person."

"The only strength he had he got from his job, from the power it gave him over the people who worked for him. He looked strong and talked tough, but all he was was a bully. There was nothing inside."

"Even so." She put her feet flat on the deck and leaned forward with her elbows on her knees, rolling her wineglass back and forth slowly between her palms. "Even a person like that might do something completely unexpected, if somebody pushed him hard enough."

"True. If Bonham really had something on Norris, and if he tried to use it to get Norris fired from his cushy new job, *then* Norris might go after him. That's why I don't say one-hundred percent 'no' to Norris." Tony smiled down at Pat. "I guess that's a long way of saying you might be right, that Norris could've killed him. But Bonham'd really have to have him by the tender clackers and be ready to chop 'em off."

Tony tilted his head back and drained his glass, then reached for Pat's glass. "Anyway, Norris is gone. More wine?"

"No. Thank you." Her answer was quiet against the background of surf, her face a soft glow in the fading light. She shifted again in her chair. "Then there's who—Deb Thomas?" She added with a rush, "I know you're heading for Paul Taylor but what about Deb Thomas?"

Tony shrugged and said, "I didn't pick Taylor out ahead of time. It's just that everything leads to him, that's all. *My* version of everything, at least." He shrugged again. "I could be wrong. I don't think so, though. As for Deb, I doubt that she's physically strong enough. And—"

"Really?" Pat swung her head around and looked up. Her voice was slow and skeptical. "I don't know. That's a pretty self-reliant young woman there! You heard what she said about taking five years of judo. And karate? Those so-called 'martial arts.' Aren't they used for *more* than self-defense?"

He let a silence hang there in the almost-dark before he said, "*And*, as I was about to say—"

Pat ducked her head and pretended chagrin. "Sorry." She got to her feet and began pacing the deck in front of Tony, slowly, five steps east, five steps west.

"And," he went on, "supposing that Deb could have done it. Physically. I can't think of any reason why she *would* have done it."

"Well, what if Bonham really had something on Norris and somehow—I know this stretches your theory a little—but suppose that somehow he got together with Deb and told her about it. And *she* went to Norris, confronted him with it, and—"

"Why would she do that? All she had to do was go to her father."

Pat suddenly stopped pacing and the wood deck thumped as though she'd stamped a foot on it. "Suppose she didn't *want* to go to her father! *Or* to Paul Taylor *or* to you or any other man. Suppose she wanted to do it, by God, *herself!*"

They looked at each other quietly across the dark deck. After a couple of seconds Tony said, "Okay. But how did she get to the studio?"

"I don't know. But isn't it *possible* that *she* could have done it?"

"Yes. It's possible. I just don't think of women that way."

"I know," she said. She reached up and touched his cheek. "I know. But remember Lady Macbeth? Or should we start with the Bible?"

He shook his head. "No." He put his arm around her shoulders and they stood together in the moonlight. "What this means, though, is that Musket Beach will be host next week to two suspicious beauties."

"Is Pomeroy right? Is the case really closed? Can't the police here do *something?*"

"I don't have any answers. But I'll start looking, come Monday morning."

TWENTY

Monday-Thursday — Musket Beach

TONY MADE THREE telephone calls on Monday morning, to a parcel delivery service in Portland, to the United States Attorney's office in Portland, and to the San Francisco advertising agency in which Gary Bonham had been a partner, where Tony talked with Abe Arthur.

Monday afternoon, Abe Arthur called back. "Found it, just where you thought. And you were right."

"Does it say what I thought it would say?"

"Right. Sleazy bastard."

"Well, he's no longer with us."

"A sleazy bastard, dead or alive."

"Can you make a copy for me?"

"Done. But they can't ship it till tomorrow morning."

"That's okay. They only make deliveries to Musket Beach twice a week. Tuesday and Thursday. So if it's in Portland tomorrow, it's sure to get here on Thursday."

"Twice a week?"

"Abe, in a garden spot of the universe, we live life at a slower pace."

"Suppose you need something in a hurry?"

"One of the first things you learn about life in a garden spot is that you never need things in a hurry."

"Jesus!"

"Right! One of our teachers."

"Talk to you later."

"Thanks for your help."

"Twice a week!"

Tony put the phone down on Abe's mumbling.

Late Monday night he picked it up again and placed his first call to Inspector Vincent Pomeroy in London.

EXCEPT FOR ASKING two or three questions, Pat listened to Tony's side of the phone calls without comment. She read. They walked on the beach. They went into town for dinner a couple of times. They saw the play at the Musket Beach Little Theater.

ON THURSDAY NIGHT he called London the second time and got the answers to some of the questions he'd asked on his first call.

Yes, the staff at the hotel bar remembered Mr. Bonham drinking heavily on the Monday afternoon.

Yes, the staff remembered seeing Mr. Bonham and Mr. Taylor together.

No, Miss Thomas wasn't with them at any time, although she did hurry out of the hotel just as they drove away in Taylor's car. The doorman put her in a cab. He got the impression she might have been following them.

"One additional point," Pomeroy said, "something that hasn't come out before."

"Norris?"

"Yes, as you suggested in your previous call. We were terribly remiss in not pressing the point before, but this time we asked specifically whether other Americans were in the bar while Bonham was there.

"Now, two witnesses place Norris in the bar at the same time, sitting in a corner behind a newspaper. The barman and a waiter both mentioned him, thinking it a bit odd that, since the Americans had arrived in the same party, they didn't get together. All the while Bonham was drinking and nattering on, Norris didn't stir. Not even when Taylor came on the scene."

"But when Taylor took Bonham away, Norris followed. Right?"

"No, sir, I'm afraid not."

"Damn."

"He followed someone else."

" 'Someone else'?"

"Miss Thomas."

TWENTY-ONE

Friday—Musket Beach

"THERE'S THE VOLCANO."

Paul Taylor waved his hand in front of Deb Thomas's nose and pointed out the right side of the airplane's windshield. Sitting in the left seat, Taylor kept the wheel pulled back a little as his Cessna rose above Portland International Airport and turned, climbing toward six thousand feet.

Deb leaned forward against her seat belt to see what he was pointing at.

His voice sounded tinny in the earphones clamped across her head. "Mount St. Helens."

Less than fifty miles north she saw a broad-based cone of a mountain, bald, plump and gray. The only other color on its bare flanks came from a few vertical strips of glacier streaked with ash.

"Eight thousand feet tall, two thousand feet shorter than she was before she erupted. Looks like a nice, symmetrical dome from here, but just over the crest on the other side the top of the mountain isn't there any more. When we come back from the coast, if we have time and if you're interested, we'll fly around it and you'll see the crater.''

He broke off his constant search of the sky to glance across the cockpit at the back of her head. ''Can you hear me? Too loud? Too soft?''

Still leaning forward, Deb twisted her neck around and tapped her headset. She nodded yes, she could hear, and then shook her head no, the volume wasn't too loud or too soft.

Taylor kept his eyes on her. ''Good,'' he said. She looked tired, pale, dark under the eyes.

He reached across and twisted the tiny, foam-covered microphone attached to her headset so that it hung in front of her lips. ''The microphone works,'' he grinned. He'd been trying to get a spark out of her ever since she'd walked off her jet from San Francisco into his big bundle of flowers but nothing made a connection.

''I hate these things,'' she said. When she heard her own voice through the earphones, Deb shivered her shoulders and made a sour face. ''Not the things. The way they make me sound.''

He went back to his scan, swiveling his head, on the watch for other traffic. ''Nothing could make you sound bad.''

She gave him a sideways glance.

He smiled again. ''Of course, you don't *look* too good.''

"Thank you."

"You look worried."

"I *am* worried."

"Not about my flying, I hope. I've been doing it for twenty years, and so far I've always made an equal number of takeoffs and landings."

"No. You know."

"I know. And I keep telling you, there's no need to worry about what happened in London. But we'll talk about it when we get to my place." He touched her shoulder. "So just relax. We'll be at the coast in less than an hour."

After Deb scooted back in her seat and folded her hands in her lap, he said, "Good. Should I stop with my 'tour director' spiel or would you like to hear more?"

She raised her left hand a little and made a circular motion.

He caught the motion out of the corner of his eyes. "Go ahead? Good. Well. You see Mount St. Helens off to the right. And if you look past St. Helens, farther north in Washington, you can see Mount Rainier, not far from Seattle. And when we took off, you saw Mount Hood. Hood's in Oregon. They're all part of the Cascade Range that runs from California through Oregon and Washington up to Canada. They're mostly ten thousand, eleven thousand, twelve thousand feet high."

Taylor glanced over at Deb but her head was turned away toward the right-hand window of the plane and tilted back, resting against the back of the seat.

"That big river down there is the Columbia, the dividing line between Oregon and Washington. The smaller river coming in from the south? That's the Willamette, and be sure to pronounce it that way in your meetings next week—'Will-AM-ette.'" He smiled and added, "Don't say 'WillaMET' or you'll never sell another loaf of bread in Oregon. And be sure you say 'OR-ygun' and not 'O-Ree-GAWN.'"

He smiled at her. Still no response and still she kept her head turned toward the window.

"Behind us, stretching from the Cascade Range back to the east, the state is very dry. Part of it's desert. But from the Cascades west, the part we're flying over, it's so different that you think you're in another part of the world, green and lush, lots of water, very fertile farms, forests as far as you can see. Obviously."

Deb's head, resting against the back of her seat, turned toward him and he looked around. Her eyes were closed, her lips parted, her breathing deep and regular.

He reached out and cut the sound to her headset.

"And our tour continues westward," he muttered to himself, "toward the Coast Range of mountains—impressive, but nothing like the Cascades—where our enchanting tale will end at our next port of call, the charming village of Musket Beach on the beautiful Oregon coast, as the sun slowly sinks in the east."

He looked at Deb. Not a flicker.

TWENTY-TWO

Friday—Musket Beach (continued)

DEB DIDN'T OPEN her eyes until after Taylor had landed the plane at the airstrip outside Seashore Village. She finally stirred at the sound of the engine changing pitch when he throttled down and taxied toward his tie-down spot.

"Some landing," she said.

"Some sleeper."

She dozed again during the fifteen-minute drive to his house just north of Musket Beach.

But her eyes opened wide after one long look at the view from his living room.

"This is almost unbelievable," she said. "It's like a dream."

He waved his hand, back and up, toward the slope of Mount Kenai. "It gets even better up the mountain."

"Couldn't be. Show me." She smiled at him and her eyes came to life, still red-rimmed, but brighter.

"Now? I thought you were tired."

"Feeling much better. That little nap in the airplane helped a lot."

"Put you right to sleep, did I?—"

"I'm sorry."

"—with my little travelogue? Maybe I should tape it and sell it, a substitute for Valium."

"I said I was sorry."

"I can hear the commercials now. 'Kick the Valium habit, friends, with *Taylor's Torpid Travelogue*.'"

"Come *on*." She slapped the back of her hand against his chest. "Show me where to change. I'll put some slacks on and change my shoes and let's go."

"You're sure you feel up to this?"

"Positive. I want to see that view."

THEY CLIMBED NEARLY a thousand feet. They climbed through a dark forest of fir and spruce, passed into dappled scrub pine, Scotch broom, and lupine and finally, in brilliant sunshine, scuffed over loose, dusty stones and scattered patches of matted chickweed till they stopped a few feet below the crest on a wide strip of bare basalt. The brown rock was chipped and cracked, but the wind and the rain had buffed it to a fine gloss. Reflecting the angled afternoon sunlight, it glowed like a lamp on the mountainside.

Deb sat on the warm stone and looked south to forests, mountains, beach, surf, ocean and sky as far as she could see. "The edge of the continent," she said. Her voice was almost a whisper. "Incredible." She wrapped her arms around her knees. "If the climb doesn't do it, this view will take your breath away."

Taylor stood looking down at her. On the slope, her eyes were not far below his. "You," he said. "You are incredible. You become your surroundings. Your eyes are even a different color."

"Flattery. Plain, bald, beautiful flattery." She smiled. "And I love it."

"That's the first time you've smiled today."

"I know," she said, and the smile began to fade.

She reached out and tugged at the leg of his pants, then held her hand out. He took her hand and wrapped his own around it as he sat down beside her. "I haven't smiled in quite a while. Even my dad mentioned it." She smiled again but this time it was quick and grim. "He thinks I'm feeling bad because of what happened to Chet Norris." With her free hand she scooped up a pebble and flung it downhill. "If he only knew."

Taylor massaged her hand in his. "He'll never know. There's no need for him to know. And I tell you once again." He tapped her hand in time with his words. "Do. Not. Worry."

"I know." Deb bobbed her head up and down. "I know. But I can't stop." She pulled her hand away and sat up, resting her forearms on her knees. She looked away to Musket Beach and the sea. "And what a setting to talk about our sordid problems."

"What problems!" His voice was so loud that she almost jumped. More calmly he said, "There are no problems. Remember?—the British police have closed the case. Buttoned it up. The fact that Tony Pratt is fussing around with a few theories doesn't mean a thing. There's nothing he can do— nothing anyone else can do, either."

Taylor's reassuring voice trailed away down the mountainside and seemed to take Deb's spirit with it.

Her shoulders sagged. She dropped her head to her chest. "I wish I hadn't given you the key. I wish I'd just thrown it away. Dropped it in the tube station. Tossed it away in the park. Anything." She raised her head and spoke to the sky. "If I'd thrown it away, no one would ever have—"

"No. I'm the one who screwed up with the key. I shouldn't have given it to Pratt. If I hadn't tried to be such a smartass, he'd never even have got *this* close."

"But it's not just the key." She turned and looked at him with tears in her eyes. "Really, Paul, what keeps me awake nights is, there *must* be somebody else who knows about the—"

"Deb, stop. Please." He held her chin with his thumb and forefinger. "You're losing sleep and driving yourself crazy for no reason."

"No reason!"

"All right, then." He let his hand slide down her arm till he wrapped her hand in his. "There *was* good reason. But it's gone. What happened, happened. Over there. Now we're over here. So it's finished and there's nothing anybody can do about it."

"Are you sure?"

"Yes."

"What about Tony?"

"I told you. There's nothing *anybody* can do. Besides, he's only guessing. He doesn't have any proof."

"Is he guessing right?"

"No. Close, but no. And even if he gets it right, we're in the U.S. of A. What's he gonna do about it? *Nada.*"

Taylor stood up, pulling Deb to her feet. "So try to get it out of your head," he said. "Come on, let me show you the rest of my view."

He put his arm around her waist, watching for Deb's reaction as they reached the top of the mountain.

She looked north and smiled. Pine-covered hills, tawny beaches, blue and white surf ran in a ragged line north to Oregon's border, where the Columbia River poured into the Pacific. From beneath a bluff on the Oregon side, a narrow string of a bridge stretched over the river's broad brownish mouth and anchored at the foot of another tall bluff on the Washington side.

The fir-topped bluff fell away to the left, sloping to the ocean's edge, where the gleaming white sands of the Long Beach peninsula pointed north to the Olympic Peninsula and Canada.

Taylor draped his arm around Deb's shoulder, grinning. "Whenever I come up here, I always think that I can look south and see California and look north and see Canada."

"It's marvelous." Deb's voice was almost a breath. She turned her head around to look south, then out to sea, and then north again. "Absolutely marvelo—"

Suddenly she caught her breath and spun away, into Taylor, pushing backward from the crest.

She'd looked down and discovered that she was standing on the edge of a cliff. There was nothing in front of her. The mountainside was just a shell. To the west there was the ocean. There was forest on the south side. On the east was the rest of the continent. But five feet away there was nothing but air.

Deb grabbed Taylor's arm, squeezed it, before she looked down again. Far below, she saw little men in puffing yellow machines ripping the mountain apart.

A quarry. A sheer drop of two thousand feet to jagged rock and stone.

TWENTY-THREE

Saturday—Musket Beach

TONY BACKED the Volvo out of the visitors' parking space in front of Musket Beach City Hall. Sitting quietly beside him, Pat didn't say a word. But he knew she was watching him. Even with his head turned away to look over his shoulder, he knew she was watching. He felt her eyes and almost heard her voice.

He straightened the wheels, heading for the parking lot entrance. He resettled in his seat and let his hand drop down over the right-hand pocket of his safari jacket to make sure it was buttoned, to tuck the shirt of the jacket under his leg to keep it from falling off the side of the seat. He didn't look at Pat until he'd turned right on Main for the short drive to Cedar Street—Cedar led up the foot of the mountain to Paul Taylor's driveway—then he glanced over and said, "Go ahead. What is it you want to say?"

"Tell me again why we're going up there. And don't tell me 'lunch.'"

"You know why we're going."

"Okay, then explain to me why we stopped at the police station on the way."

"You're frowning. Don't frown when you're getting a free lunch."

She turned away. "And if stopping at the police station had anything to do with Paul Taylor, don't bother to explain. Just turn around and let's get *out* of here."

"C'mon. I just wanted to see Chief Barrett for a second—tell him he might be getting a phone call or two from Portland."

"*Chief* Barrett? I thought he was *Officer* Barrett."

"The city sprung for another cop."

"We now have two policemen?"

Tony nodded. "And Barry's the chief." He turned left onto Cedar, shifting down for the winding climb to Taylor's driveway.

"Did you tell him that you know where he could catch a killer?" She looked out at thick mounds of blackberry vines growing between the alders alongside the road.

"We don't *know* that."

"You believe it."

"I could be wrong."

"*I* believe it."

He shrugged. "Maybe *you're* the one who's—"

"I'm not."

"Okay."

He shifted again and turned right into Taylor's driveway. He knew it was Taylor's driveway. As he'd said to Pat, "Who else would stencil his house number across it in big block numerals to make it look like a runway?"

Tony stopped where the drive leveled off beside the house, set the brake, cut the ignition, and turned in his seat to face Pat. "Okay," he said again, "let's assume we're right. Suppose Taylor killed Gary Bonham—"

Pat shook her head.

"All right. Deborah Thomas. Suppose Deborah Thomas killed Gary Bonham. Whoever. Whomever. *Anybody* who did it is sure they're in the clear. They heard Inspector Pomeroy say officially that *Norris* did it and then met an 'untimely death.' The police were satisfied, they closed the drawer, and that was that."

Tony bobbed his head toward the house. "So the people in there don't care *what* we do or say. Taylor, at least, doesn't care. I know for a fact that he can sit and listen to me theorize till it comes out the ying-yang. 'Very interesting, *yawn*.' Couldn't be less impressed. Which means that we don't have anything to worry about."

"Now wait a minute." Pat frowned at her husband. "Not very long ago you were saying that there might be a killer running around in Musket Beach and the idea made you very nervous."

He held up an index finger. "Yes, but." He dropped his hand and let it rest on her knee. "What I'm trying to say is that it finally, *finally* occurred to me *why* Taylor doesn't care one diddley flop about anything we do or say. Pomeroy told him it was over. Therefore, Taylor thinks it's over. Therefore, even if we come up with something against him, *he* believes that there's nothing we can do about it.

"Where can we take it? The local police?—We must be kidding. The feds?—Who feds, what feds, which feds? London?—'Sorry, old chap, but didn't you hear that file drawer when it closed?'

"Therefore," he tapped her knee with the flat of his hand, "to wind up this little rationale, my bet is that we can go in, have lunch, talk about the case any way we want, and still not worry about getting dropped in the ocean."

"Hope you're right," she said with a sigh. "But I'd feel safer if—"

A voice shouted, "Hey!"

They both jumped and looked out. Paul Taylor stood watching from the veranda that ran along the side of his house, one hand cupped around his mouth, his other hand raised to wave a warning finger as he said loudly, "There are people who might say that you two are getting too old to sit in the car and neck."

Tony turned to open his door. As he swung, the right-hand pocket of his safari jacket slid off the seat. The lumpy weight in the pocket tugged the side of his jacket down and made it sag off his right shoulder.

"What's that in your pocket!" Pat's eyes bugged and her voice was a scratchy whisper. "Good lord! Is that a—"

Tony didn't answer.

Watching Taylor, he got out of the car and said loudly, "Luckily, I don't know *anyone* who'd use the word 'neck.'"

"Well," Taylor answered quickly, "perhaps you'd prefer—"

"Never mind!" Pat stepped out and looked at him across the roof of the car. "I've heard a few of your alternative terms. 'Neck' is acceptable."

"Ah, ha!" Taylor slapped his hands together and grinned at Pat as Deb Thomas came out of the house and stood beside him. "The principal Pratt is heard from."

Pat raised her hand, palm out. "There are no principals here," she said, walking around the car to Tony. Her gesture could have been a wave or it could have been a warning.

"What you see here is an equal opportunity organization," Tony said.

He took Pat's hand and they went up the wooden steps together. "We have principles but we have no principals."

"Well!" Deb said with a mock frown. "I may have fallen in with the wrong crowd. This sounds like a word-play afternoon." Then she smiled and held out her hand to Pat. "Hello, again."

Pat returned her smile as they shook hands and Taylor said, "No, no more word-play from now on. Straight talk only. And since we all know what we're gonna talk about, let's set the ground rules right now. Okay?"

He looked at the others, then focused on Tony. "Fine."

"Okay. So let's have no phoney baloney. Each of us can say what's on our mind. In a calm and forthright fashion. Clear the air. And get this whole shitaree settled without anybody getting excited. Okay?"

Taylor leaned back against the railing and glanced around. The others nodded and Tony said, "Sounds fair enough."

Pat moved her head as if to speak, then apparently changed her mind, but not before Taylor caught the movement. "Go ahead and say it. Whatever. We just agreed on that."

"I think this is pretty strange."

Taylor grinned. "I think you think everything I do is strange."

"Aside from that." Pat smiled her bright business smile. "And no word-play. Remember?"

Her smile disappeared and she said, "Inviting us to lunch to talk about Gary Bonham's murder—in which we are all intimately involved—is very strange." Her eyes threw a dart at Tony. "What's even stranger is, we came."

Before Tony could say anything, Taylor smiled and blurted, "That's the point! We were all, as you say, 'intimately involved' with Bonham's *death*, but *nobody* here was involved with his *murder*, despite Tony's theories. That's why I invited you. I want that cleared up." He reached out to Deb. "For her sake."

Deb moved over to stand beside him along the railing.

He took her left hand in his and slid his right hand across her shoulder, under her hair. She lowered her head. He slowly massaged the back of her neck while he went on speaking, his voice now low and quiet, just low enough and just quiet enough to still be heard over the wind's gentle movement through the fir trees.

"Deb doesn't need anyone to speak for her, as you know." His eyes went back and forth between

Tony and Pat. "But ever since I told her about this 'theory' of yours, she's really been strung out. Tense. Worried. Afraid of your crazy ideas and afraid that somebody else might take you *seriously*."

He slid his big hand all the way across her back and wrapped it around her shoulder. "That's why we're here. To get this all out in the open. To get it out in the open, so I can blow it away right in front of her. To prove that she can put it all behind her and have some peace of mind again."

With his arm still around Deb, Taylor pushed away from the railing and said, "Now, with that little speech out of the way, let's go sit down and talk this out."

He led them along the veranda toward a cluster of redwood chairs and lounges on the ocean side of the house.

Tony and Pat trailed behind, far enough so that Tony could take Pat's hand and say quietly, "Some day I'd like to write a movie for that guy."

"You think he was acting?"

"Robert Duvall couldn't have done it any better."

"Really?"

"Absolutely."

TWENTY-FOUR

Saturday—Musket Beach (continued)

SUDDENLY TAYLOR SPUN around and threw his hands up. "Hold it! Marvelous idea!"

He stabbed a thick index finger at Pat. "You say I have 'an impulse for the dramatic'? Try this. Instead of sitting down here, as pleasant as it is, let's go up there!"

He grinned and swung his arm around in a gesture that swept across the view from his deck and ended with his finger pointing to the top of Mount Kenai. "Talk about clearing the air!"

Deb seemed surprised but the expression on her face was no match for Pat's. "Are you out of your mind?"

She turned to Tony but he shrugged and said, "Why not? Besides, I've never seen the view from up there. Have you?"

Taylor was rubbing his hands together. "Tremendous idea! 'Go tell it on the mountain,'" he sang, "and leave that sucker there!"

Pat ignored him, her attention still on Tony. At the same time, Tony seemed to be ignoring Pat. He turned away to gaze along the veranda toward the driveway and their Volvo.

"Don't worry about your car," Taylor said. "Nobody'll bother it. I leave mine in the driveway all the time."

Tony started back toward the steps. "I think I'll be sure it's locked, just in case."

"Tony!" Pat somehow packed irritation, disbelief, curiosity, and an order to halt in those two syllables.

"Won't take a minute," he said over his shoulder. "Go ahead." He motioned toward the rear of the house. "I'll meet you around there."

For a second Pat stood still, seeming to study the back of Tony's head or to feel the air currents as he moved away. Then she nodded once, slowly, and said to Taylor. "Okay. If that's where he'll meet us, let's go there."

A FEW MINUTES later they were climbing the slope, with Deb and Taylor leading the way.

Pat asked Tony, "You're sure about this?"

He shrugged and answered, "Life is a gamble. Who can be sure?"

She looked at him out of the corner of her eye. "Shouldn't you save comments like that for the *top* of the mountain, Wise One?" She shook her head. "Anyway, that's not the answer I wanted."

"The best we can do is try to shorten the odds."

"Neither is that one."

"I think we're all right."

She was silent for a few more steps and then, "Let's turn this around."

"How?"

"You ask the questions and *I'll* give the answers."

"Let's save our breath."

After that, the only other sounds came from birds, wind, or an occasional unintelligible sentence between Taylor and Deb.

They climbed through forest, through scrub, and out above timberline. Now and then they stopped to catch their breath or to see the view or to do both.

Sometimes, after a break like that, instead of turning and facing the mountain to continue the climb, Tony and Pat walked backward up the slope. This way they watched the view expand.

It spread beyond the treetops and over Taylor's house and driveway, opening out to Musket Beach and the coastline and on south into a haze that hadn't been there yesterday.

High above the beach a wide, gauzy layer of cirrus clouds drifted inland, forecasting a weather change. Small white puffs of clouds trailed behind the cirrus in neat, orderly rows. Far away, out to sea, gigantic black-bottomed clouds sat on the horizon line like a snow-covered mountain range.

Deb Thomas stopped, leaning her hip against a dark, pitted boulder a few yards from the rock outcropping where she'd stopped the day before. She looked at Tony and Pat with an odd expression, her eyes worried but her lips trying to smile. "I think this is far enough, Tony. This should satisfy Paul's sense of the dramatic."

Tony nodded while Pat looked out over the ocean and said, "More than enough."

"Right," Tony added. He glanced to his right and down the slope as he touched Pat's elbow. "Want a boost?"

She shook her head. "I can make it." She backed against the flat-topped rock and hiked herself up, perching with one leg bent up to rest her arm on and the other leg dangling nearly to the ground.

"Perfect," Taylor said. "Deb?"

He gestured toward the boulder but she shook her head. "I'm fine right here."

"Okay." Then, as if giving him a cue, Taylor turned and pointed at Tony. "Go. Tell us on the mountain. Let Deb hear your 'scenario' or 'story treatment' or whatever."

"'Guess' is what you called it the last time we went over it," Tony said, "but it's a little more than that now."

Deb's eyes shifted nervously between Taylor and Tony.

Leaning back against the boulder beside Pat's knee, Tony repeated what he'd told Taylor in the bar.

Taylor's response was also a repetition, the same denial he'd made in the bar, including his statement that nothing could be done about it now. He seemed to be saying, in effect, "So you think you've made a case against me? So what!"

Deb Thomas listened to Tony's theory and to Taylor's defiant remarks. When they'd finished, she stood with her feet close together and crossed her arms over her chest. She shifted her eyes back and forth between Tony and Pat. "Please. Tell me, please, why can't you just let this go? It's over! Isn't it over? Didn't Inspector Pomeroy say that? Didn't he say the case is closed? Quote-unquote?"

Pat's eyes were steady on Deb. "Yes, he said that."

"But he's changed his mind," Tony added.

"He what!" Deb swung her head around and stared wide-eyed at Taylor.

Taylor let a second skip by, watching Tony. "How do you know that?" His eyes and voice were cold.

"I called him. I asked him to check with people at the hotel—bartenders, waiters and so on. I wanted to find out if they'd seen you together the afternoon he was killed."

"I *told* you," Taylor sneered. "I told you I ran into Bonham outside the bar."

Tony shook his head. "Not you and Bonham. You and Deb."

Deb seemed surprised but Taylor said quickly, "And what did Pomeroy say to that?"

"You know what he said."

"Yes!" Deb's voice was desperate. "But what difference does that make? We were coming back after lunch. We passed the bar and saw Gary inside. I told Paul that he'd been trying to talk to me about something."

"Wait a minute, wait a minute, wait a minute." Taylor put his hands on Deb's shoulders and moved her aside, so that he could stand in front of Tony. "You're getting her all upset again. For nothing. I don't know what you and Pomeroy think you're doing, but this thing is *finished*. Done. Wrapped up. He may think it's open in England, but we're over *here*."

From her seat on the rock, Pat looked at Deb and said one word. "Extradition."

Deb stared. "What?"

Pat said, "You could be sent back."

"Sent back?"

"Arrested and sent back to stand trial."

"Arrested!" Deb turned to Taylor.

"Where's the tape?" Tony snapped.

"I threw it awa—" she snapped back without thinking, then cut herself off, and her head sagged down on her chest as Taylor broke in. "What tape?"

"Bonham's," Tony said.

"There isn't any tape."

"The tape he wanted to play for Deb."

"There isn't any tape."

"Don't lie to me any more, Paul." Tony's right hand slid inside the bulging pocket of his jacket.

Taylor caught the movement. "No! Don't touch it!"

Suddenly a slender piece of gently curved bone appeared in Taylor's right hand. He pressed it with his thumb and a glittering steel blade flicked out.

The others stared as if he'd made a dragon appear.

Taylor squinted at Tony. "I told you not to touch the gun."

"Gun? What would I do with a gun?" Tony pulled his hand slowly out of his pocket and held it open. "All this is is a tape recorder." He looked at Deb. "With a copy of the tape that doesn't exist." He turned back to Taylor, shaking his head. "And

I'm surprised at you. After all your years in the business?—forgetting about the original? Even Gary Bonham remembered to make a copy of the tape and keep the original.''

''Where? Where'd you get that?''

''From his office. In San Francisco. That's where he recorded Chet Norris's phone call when Chet tried to shake him down for more money.''

Taylor waved the knife and held his other hand out. ''Give me the tape.''

''No.'' Tony looked at Deb. ''I want to play it for Deb.''

Her shoulders sagged. Her eyes were frightened, her skin as pale as the clouds. ''She says she doesn't know what's on it. But I think she does. I think you *both* know. And Gary didn't tell you—he wanted you to hear it for yourself. And the only time he could've given you the tape was the night he was killed. And the only place was *where* he was killed. So, the only way you could've got your hands on it was to take it off his body.''

Tony raised his hand and turned the little tape machine on. Chet Norris spoke from the grave, and then Gary Bonham. Deb Thomas shivered, listening to the dead.

NORRIS: It's true, my promotion to Marketing Director brings me a bigger paycheck, but it also increases my expenses. (HE LAUGHED) I'll have to move into a better apartment, drive a better car, drink a better grade of booze, buy a better class of hookers. You know how that goes. So I'll have to continue to "augment" my income.

BONHAM: I think I understand.

NORRIS: In fact, I'll have to "augment" my "augmentation," if you follow me.

BONHAM: That might be hard to do.

NORRIS: You'll find a way. You always do. Incidentally, you'd be surprised at the number of calls I've been getting from other advertising agencies. The hottest rumor on the street seems to be that I'm going to drop your shop and take our account someplace else. A couple of agencies right here in Chicago, in fact, indicated that I might find a change very advantageous. No, that isn't the word they used. What was it they said? Ah, yes. "Rewarding." They said—

"Stop it!" Deb Thomas cried. "They're all *dead!* They can't talk!" She fell to her knees behind Taylor, weeping into her hands. "They're *dead*, for God's sake!"

"Give me the tape, Pratt."

Tony yelled past Taylor. "Gary wanted your father to hear this, Deb."

"No. Please," Deb sobbed. "Don't."

Pat hopped down and started toward her.

"I said give me the tape!"

"He wanted you to tell your dad what a crook he had on his hands!"

"Stop. Stop." Hunched on the ground, she cried. "Giveittome!"

"No." Tony dropped the recorder back into his pocket. "It goes to Pomeroy."

On her way to comfort Deb, Pat rushed past Taylor. His hand shot out and grabbed her by the hair. He yanked and she screamed, bent backwards, and then fell at his feet.

"You sonofabitch!" Tony yelled, running to Pat. As he knelt beside her, Taylor took one quick step forward and kicked at his face. Tony ducked but Taylor's bootheel cracked against his skull. He grunted and fell backwards and the back of his head thumped against the rocky ground and he rolled onto his side.

Taylor stepped across Pat's body and squatted over Tony with one knee pushing down on his neck. He pressed the point of his knife against Tony's cheek while his other hand clawed at Tony's pockets. "I said gimme the tape, ya hear me? Gimme the fuckin' tape!"

Deb slowly crumpled, folded to the ground, sitting on her ankles with her hands splayed across her face, sobbing, squinting at Taylor through tight red eyes and tear-stained dirty fingers. "Paul. Stop. It's crazy. Stop. Paul."

Pat pushed herself up to her hands and knees and shook her head, a little dizzy, looking for Tony. She saw him sprawled in the dirt with Taylor kneeling on him holding a knife against his cheek. Her eyes flared and she let out a growling roar and charged, driving herself at Taylor like a football tackle.

Taylor heard Pat coming and turned, but not in time. She crashed into his side yelling "You sonofabitch!" like Tony's high-pitched echo, and when she felt her shoulder crunch his ribs, she kept yelling and pumping her legs. She knocked him off of Tony and he dropped the knife, and she fell on top of him punching, swinging, cursing, clawing, kicking. She smashed her fists and drove her knees into Taylor anywhere she could reach.

Tony raised his head and squinted through the blood dripping down from his forehead over his eyelids and lashes. He staggered to his feet wiping a sleeve across his eyes. He saw Pat spread-eagled on Taylor. He stumbled toward her, spotted the long knife glittering in the dirt and with a sweeping kick sent it clattering up the mountainside in a spout of dirt and stones. It sailed over the top just as Paul Taylor wrapped his arms around Pat, pinned hers, flipped her over and straddled her.

Stumbling forward, Tony fell across Taylor's back and hooked his left arm around his neck. He grabbed his own left wrist to tighten his hold. He scrambled to his feet, dragging Taylor away from Pat.

She rolled over and got up as Tony yanked Taylor sideways, grunting and panting. "Stop, Paul. Stop it. Look down there. In your driveway."

Pat, Deb, Taylor, Tony—they all looked down the mountain to Taylor's house. Another car was parked beside Tony and Pat's Volvo, a car with a row of red and blue lights flashing across its top.

"Musket Beach Police," Tony said, still short of breath. "Think I'd come up here? Bring my wife up here? Without some kind of backup?"

Straining against Tony's grip, Taylor rolled his head around and grunted.

Another light flashed beside the car, disappeared, came back. "Must be Barrett. Checking us through binoculars."

Taylor's body relaxed. He sagged forward a little. Behind him, Tony had to lean with him slightly to keep his grip tight. Shifting his weight, Tony was off-balance for just an instant, but in that split second Taylor grabbed his arm and the back of his head, snapped forward at the waist, and flipped him through the air.

Pat screamed again as Tony flew over Taylor's head. One foot cracked her in the shoulder and knocked her down. Tony landed on his back and bounced. His reflexes got him rolled over and up on one knee, but that's as far as he could go.

Panting, leaning on his knee, he looked for Pat and saw her scramble to her feet. Rubbing a shoulder with one hand, she started in his direction.

Taylor lunged at her, grabbed her, twisted one of her arms behind her back. Pat fought back but he spun her around and clamped her other arm as he kicked at Tony, trying to get up. His boot caught Tony in the knee and knocked him off balance again.

"Deb!" Taylor shouted. "The tape! Get the tape!"

"No!" Deb Thomas was still in the same position, on her knees in the dust with her hands covering her face. Through her dirty, tear-streaked fingers she watched Tony trying to push himself to his feet. "No!" she cried again. "Stop it!"

"Whaddaya mean, 'no'!" Taylor roared, fighting to hold on to Pat as she twisted and fought.

"Who the hell do you think I'm *doin'* this for! Get over here before he gets up!"

With tears streaming down her face, Deb struggled to her feet, all the while crying, "Stop, stop, stop."

Tony was on one knee again, panting, gulping air. "Let her go, Paul."

Clutching Pat—twisting, wiggling, turning—Taylor concentrated on Deb. "Go. Go on."

Struggling and twisting, Pat finally saw Tony out of the corner of her eye. He crouched and pulled in another lungful of air and suddenly charged, screaming as loud as he could scream.

Startled, Taylor turned and saw Tony, and then Pat shrieked right in his ear. Shocked and stunned, Taylor's grip loosened enough for Pat to jerk her elbow forward, bringing his hand around, and she bent down and sank her teeth in his wrist.

Taylor yelled and jerked away. Pat slipped to the ground. Tony slammed into Taylor with a cross-body block that drove him up the slope. Stumbling backwards, he fell against Deb and clutched at her, trying to gain his balance. "No!" she screamed. He grabbed her arm. "Stop!" She tried to yank free. He held on. She stiffened her hand and chopped his throat. Taylor made a gagging sound, released her arm, and stumbled backward off the mountain.

TWENTY-FIVE

Saturday—Musket Beach (continued)

DEB DROPPED TO her hands and knees. She held her
back straight for a few seconds and then she col-
lapsed, drained and limp. Her feet pointed down
the slope toward Taylor's house. Her left arm and
her head rolled over the rim of the mountain, her
hair cascading down, her eyes closed tight to cut out
the sight and squeeze the tears that fell and drifted
away over the quarry above his tiny body.

Tony and Pat—bleeding, limping—carefully
pulled Deb away from the mountain rim. They
staggered a few feet backward down the slope till
they bumped the solid comfort of the big, flat-
topped rock.

Then they all sat, sprawled, with their sweat-
cooled backs pressed against the warm rock, silently recovering strength and breath, waiting for
sense and reason to make their way through the
dark of this sunny day.

After a few minutes Pat said, "Barrett?"

Tony nodded and began to move. "We'd better
get down there and tell him about..." He stopped.

He couldn't say Taylor's name. He nodded again. "We'd better go. I don't think he'll come up."

They made their painful, silent way down the mountain, over the rock and the scrub and through the cool, green woods.

Barrett met them in the clearing above Taylor's house. The second he saw them stumble out of the woods, he clicked his radio on and called for an ambulance from the clinic in Seashore Village.

Pat was limping so badly that he almost carried her across the clearing and the driveway. Tony and Deb tried to support each other. All three were exhausted by the time they reached the front of the house, where they slumped on the steps while Barrett got his first aid kit out of his police car and towels and a pan of water from the house.

After a few minutes of Barrett's care Tony sat on the top step, pressing a damp cloth against his bloody forehead with his left hand.

Pat sat two steps lower, resting her head on his knee as his other hand gently petted the back of her head.

Deb stood behind them on Taylor's veranda, leaning against one of the pillars, shaking her head whenever Barrett offered a bandage, a Band-Aid or a damp cloth.

So Barrett crouched in front of Pat with his first aid kit and his radio. While he tried to patch a cut on her knee, he called the Oregon State Police and the medical examiner and described where to find Taylor's body.

"He told me it was Chet." Deb's voice barely cleared the squawk and static of Barrett's radio.

Tony and Barrett looked up at her. She sagged against the pillar and tears rolled slowly down the dirty streaks on her face. "Over and over, he told me it was Chet. He said that Chet Norris killed Gary. Because Gary'd made that tape. And he was gonna use it to get Chet fired."

Tony shook his head. "Impossible. How would Norris know about the tape? *Nobody* knew about it except Gary. Until he told you. And then Paul."

Without raising her head from Tony's knee, Pat said, "Must've made him feel pretty cocky when Norris got hit by that truck. Thought he was home free."

"No!" Deb took everybody by surprise with the force she put behind that one syllable. After that her voice dropped back, barely audible as the ambulance siren came up the hill. "No! That's one thing he never *did* feel. 'Home free.' He felt like an outsider all his life. He acted like somebody with the world by the tail, but he was acting all the time."

The ambulance turned up the driveway. The siren cut off and the whine ground down to a growl.

"Acting all the time. To Paul it was all bullshit. *He* knew most people didn't want to be around him. *He* knew they all felt just like Chet Norris. He was a 'freak.' They'd let him in long enough to spend his talent or his money and then they'd slam the door on the little freak."

She crossed her arms over her chest. "How do you handle a lifetime of that?" Tears streamed down her face. "He gave it right back. Bullshit for bullshit. Except this time. *One time* he tries to do something for somebody. Tries to *help* somebody. Tries to protect *me*. And what happens?"

She turned and threw her arms around the pillar and hugged it and closed her eyes and screamed, "Oh shit, Paul Taylor!"

TWENTY-SIX

Sunday Morning—Musket Beach

CHIEF BARRETT stopped on the top step and surveyed the people on the front deck of Tony and Pat's beach cabin.

Pat stood in the doorway wearing shorts, a polo shirt, bandages taped over the knuckles on both hands, and an Ace bandage wrapped around her right knee, which she kept straight when she stepped out onto the deck on her single crutch.

Tony sat in a director's chair with his feet up on the railing. He turned to look at Barrett out of two black eyes. A big square of gauze covered the center of his forehead and smaller bandages were taped to both elbows.

Deborah Thomas had slept on the living room couch and was now stretched out on a deck lounge in the shade of the big escalonia bush that grew along one side. Deb had no noticeable wounds but her face was pale and worn. Her eyes were so red that they looked sore. The bags underneath were almost as dark as Tony's black eyes.

Barrett wagged his head and said, "This place looks like an emergency room on Saturday night. The only difference is, I don't smell the booze."

"A little early for us," Tony said, "but if you've got to have it, it's under the sink."

"Only a comment." Barrett waved a big white paper bag in each hand and asked Pat, "Where do you want this stuff?"

She pointed with her head. "Just put it on the railing and let people help themselves. Somebody'll have to bring the coffee tray."

"I'll get it." Deb rolled off the lounge and went inside.

Barrett plopped the bags on the wide top rail and started folding the tops down. "I got what I could. Not much left at the bakery at nine on a Sunday morning. Couple of Danish, couple of muffins, couple of those whatchamacallits—French biscuit things—"

"Croissants," Pat said.

"Those things."

"Good of you to bring breakfast," Tony said, starting to get up. "I'll find my wallet and—ouch!" He grabbed his back and stood, bent over.

Barrett reached out to help and Pat said, "Okay?"

"Sore!" Tony said. He straightened as much as possible and rubbed the small of his back with both hands. "Stiff and sore." He shook his head. "Fighting? At my age? Archie Moore's the only person who ever fought at my age."

Deb came back, carrying a tray of cups and a coffee pot. "Who's Archie Moore?"

Creaking, Tony turned to Pat. "See? Archie and me, forgotten by time and youth. Let's find some money to pay Chief Barrett for these breakfast rolls."

Barrett flapped a hand and said, "Forget it. The city's buyin' breakfast, so I can hear the rest of the story. I've got a body to explain, and I've got to explain the phone calls I've been getting from Portland and London and wherever." He pulled out his notebook and boosted himself up on the flat top rail.

"Okay. Thank the city." Tony picked up a blueberry muffin and leaned back against the railing. "Where were we before the medics took us away and fixed us up?"

"You'd started to tell him about Paul," Pat said.

Tony put the muffin down on the railing, untasted. He looked straight at Barrett, and all the time he talked, he never once looked at Deb Thomas.

"Paul Taylor killed a man," he said. "A man named Gary Bonham. In London. I don't think he meant to do it. I think he lost his temper, went out of control. He was extremely strong. Before he re-alized it, he'd hit Bonham several times. Hard. So hard he broke his ribs and stopped his heart.

"And why did he lose his temper? Bonham wanted to involve this young lady"—Tony didn't look at Deb; he waved a hand in her direction and she stared blankly out to sea—"in stopping a shakedown scheme. Taylor didn't want her in-volved. Taylor told Bonham, a couple of times, to keep her out of it. Bonham refused.

"Taylor tried to change his mind one last time. Somehow he got Bonham to go to the studio—maybe he said he wanted to hear the tape himself, maybe he said he'd show Bonham how to patch it into a phone line and play it back to the States—I don't know, but they were together in the studio. And Bonham still said no, he wanted Deb involved in it. And that's when Taylor lost his temper. They fought, Taylor punched him and kept on punch-ing, and killed him."

Deb stood and walked into the cabin. After a glance at Tony, Pat leaned on her crutch and stumped in behind her.

"And all he was trying to do," Tony said softly, "was to protect Deb."

Barrett stopped writing. "They were in the stu-dio? He left the body there?"

"He stuffed the body behind the sound effects door—"

Barrett looked at him.

"—I'll explain it later—he stuffed it behind the sound effects door, where it was found later.

"Now, here I'm guessing but I think I'm close: after he hid the body, he started back out of the studio and suddenly there was Chet Norris, the shakedown artist, walking through the reception area. Suddenly an idea flashed in Taylor's head.

"He went back to the hotel, picked up Deb for the evening recording session, and told her he'd seen Norris following Bonham. So when he and Deb got to the studio and found everybody standing around Bonham's body, all he could do was act surprised and all she could do was go along with it. He couldn't say that he'd seen Norris there, because that would've put him at the scene, too."

Pat and her crutch thumped out onto the deck again. "Deb wanted to lie down. Headache. I gave her a couple of aspirin and I told her to use our bedroom."

"Fine."

"Did you tell him about the tape?"

"Not yet. The tape and the key." Tony looked at Barrett. "There was a tape—an audio cassette of the shakedown demand. And there was a key to the studio. Bonham had both. They should have been on his body.

"If Norris had killed him, obviously, he'd have removed the evidence against himself—the tape of his phone conversation with Bonham. But there was no reason for him to take the key.

"Taylor, on the other hand, had the key. So my hunch was, he'd also taken the tape. Which Deb later confirmed. Which confirmed my hunch that Taylor had killed him."

Pat hobbled across to get some coffee. Barrett put his notebook down and poured.

"There's something I'd like to know, and I don't know if anyone will ever be able to tell me." She nodded thanks to Barrett for pouring her coffee and said, "And this is something you'll never be able to put in your notebook." She looked at Tony. "When I was in the studio, before all the horror broke out, whose footsteps did I hear? Who was in there with me, not saying a word?"

Barrett gave Pat a puzzled look and then joined her in staring at Tony.

"Damned if I know." He shrugged. "But my guess is it was Norris. Either just nosing around and not wanting to be seen just nosing around. Or else he nosed around, saw Bonham's body, and ducked out, afraid to be seen anywhere near it, because he'd be considered a prime suspect after the way he'd acted at the morning session.''

Pat sipped her coffee. "Well. That's as close as we can get, hey?"

"'fraid so."

"Well. I'm probably going to wonder about those footsteps for a long time."

Barrett flipped his notebook closed. "Try not to think about it," he smiled at Pat. "And thanks for filling me in," he said to Tony.

"Glad to." He held out his hand. "Glad you were there!"

Pat touched Barrett's sleeve. "And we appreciate the breakfast rolls."

"Think nothing of it," he said. He peeked into one of the white bags. "Why doesn't somebody eat that marionberry Danish?"

Tony's eyes lit up. "*Marion*berry? Why didn't somebody say there was marionberry in there? Oregon's the only place in the *world* you can get marionberries."

"Oh, would you like this?" Pat took the sweet roll out of the bag and held it in her hand. She winked at Barrett before she looked at Tony. "I'll split it with you. On one condition. No, you can have the whole thing, on one condition."

"Name it."

"Never, never get us involved in anything like this again."

"You got it."

Crutch in one hand and marionberry roll in the other, Pat thumped across the deck to Tony. "Fat chance," she said.

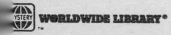

Take 3 books and a surprise gift FREE

SPECIAL LIMITED-TIME OFFER

Mail to: The Mystery Library™
3010 Walden Ave.
P.O. Box 1867
Buffalo, N.Y. 14269-1867

YES! Please send me 3 free books from the Mystery Library™ and my free surprise gift. Then send me 3 mystery books, first time in paperback, every month. Bill me only $3.69 per book plus 25¢ delivery and applicable sales tax, if any*. There is no minimum number of books I must purchase. I can always return a shipment at your cost simply by dropping it in the mail, or cancel at any time. Even if I never buy another book from The Mystery Library™, the 3 free books and surprise gift are mine to keep forever.   415 BPY A.

Name _____ (PLEASE PRINT) _____

Address _____ Apt.

City _____ State _____

*Terms and prices subject to change without notice. N.Y. residents add applicable sales tax. This offer
limited to one order per household and not valid to present subscribers.
© 1990 Worldwide Library.   MYS.

A Sheila Travis Mystery

MURDER

PATRICIA
HOUCK
SPRINKLE

on Peachtree Street

First
Time In
Paperback

NO MORE MR. NICE GUY

Prominent television personality Dean Anderson was as popular as he was respected, but he had incurred a good deal of animosity among family, friends and co-workers. Though the police are willing to rule his shooting death a suicide, his old friend Sheila Travis is not.

Because of meddling Aunt Mary, Sheila gets involved in finding Dean's killer. No easy task with a long list of suspects that includes a resentful ex-wife, an enraged daughter, a jealous co-worker, a spurned admirer, a mobster with a grudge. The truth goes deeper than either Mary or Sheila suspects. And it may prove equally fatal.

Available in November at your favorite retail stores.

Corporate Bodies

SIMON BRETT

First Time in Paperback

A
CHARLES
PARIS
MYSTERY

By the author of *Mrs. Pargeter's Package*

Surviving thirty years of an actor's fluctuating fortunes, Charles Paris had played many roles. But until now, a starring role as a forklift driver in a corporate video had yet to grace his résumé. Costumed in coveralls, he read his lines with finesse and his performance for Delmoleen foods was flawless. But the finale was murder.

A young woman is crushed to death with the forklift while the crew is at lunch. Industrial accident...or murder? Paris suspects a cover-up. The whole company atmosphere is troubling: the happy Delmoleen family seems riddled with mockery, jealousy, lust, envy. And secrets that may make this performance Charles's last.

"The most engaging new murder-solver in recent years has been Simon Brett's Charles Paris." —*Los Angeles Times*

Available in October at your favorite retail stores.